Totally Bound Publishing books by Raven McAllan:

Diomhair Volume One
Secrets Shared
Secrets Uncovered

Diomhair Volume Two
Secrets Remembered
Secrets Dispatched

DIOMHAIR
Volume Two

Secrets Remembered

Secrets Dispatched

RAVEN MCALLAN

Diomhair Volume Two
ISBN # 978-1-78430-488-1
©Copyright Raven McAllan 2015
Cover Art by Posh Gosh ©Copyright 2015
Interior text design by Claire Siemaszkiewicz
Totally Bound Publishing

SECRETS
REMEMBERED

Dedication

To Jenny, who sees my mistakes and sorts them, and
to Paul, who has to tame the dust bunnies.

Chapter One

The thought of the luxury of an evening to himself wasn't lost on Aidan Jefferies. He stretched back in his office chair and wriggled his tight shoulders. He needed a ten-mile run or a massage. Or a good workout with a sub. No not *a* sub, *his* sub, he corrected himself.

As he was damned sure he'd not fit time for the run into his schedule in the near future, and was currently sub-less without anyone on the horizon to change that, he'd have to sort out a massage sometime soon. He needed to de-kink. Well not de-kink exactly. He sniggered to himself. There was about a cat in hell's chance of that, but definitely de-knot his muscles. However, not that evening. He intended those hours to be lazy, kick back and relax ones. No massage, no companion, no thinking about work, only chilling.

Aidan glanced at the clock. Three hours and counting before he could lock his office door, get on his motorbike and ride the seven miles home. He checked the specification he'd written up, pressed send on his computer and made a note of what he'd done. There was nothing outstanding or urgent that had to be addressed there and then. His mind made up, Aidan turned on his intercom.

"Jacks?"

"She's left for hot sex with her man. This is a recording." His PA's voice came over the line. "All queries can be sorted tomorrow. If she can walk." The staccato voice stopped. "Hi, Ade, what's up?" They didn't stand on ceremony.

"Not a lot. Just get as much done as you can so we can clock off early. I reckon we need it."

"Too right. Give me time to beautify myself, eh? Shugie's home tonight." Shugie, otherwise known as Hugh, was her husband. He worked away a lot of the time. "Ah shit, hold on, that's the phone. Let me get rid of whoever it is. How dare they ring when we're going to dog off?" The intercom went dead.

Aidan shook his head. Dog off? That was an expression he hadn't heard for years. Why not skiving or playing hooky? She'd never change. Aidan took a swig of water and contemplated the evening ahead. He'd earmarked a steak and a good robust red wine for dinner, along with a gritty drama he'd recorded a few nights previously. He might even stretch to a sticky toffee pudding for dessert. Pure pig-out indulgence. Then it was going to be slouch on the sofa time, and watch hot women and steely-eyed men dice with death, and each other. Right until the credits rolled on a satisfactory ending, be it happy or not.

He wasn't needed that evening at Diomhair, a private BDSM club based in a rebuilt Scottish castle not far from where he lived. It was the place where he worked for pleasure and not necessity. Diomhair was proving to be very popular, and he was more than glad to lend a hand when necessary, over and above his allocated shifts, both as a dungeon master and a Dom. He blessed the day he'd discovered it and its owners. They had become more than good friends. In fact, they were, he acknowledged, a lifeline at times, and he never minded pulling an extra shift or doing a nice knife or wax demonstration for them.

The phone rang and he sighed. Obviously Jackie hadn't managed to fob off whoever was on the line. He hoped it wasn't going to stop them leaving early. Why did the ring sound ominous? Was it because a phone call might delay that perfect moment when he felt like a school kid playing hooky? Why it should hit him like that he had no idea. After all, Aidan was his own boss, and only had himself and Jackie to consider. She deserved time off. Over all the long and lean months she'd given him her support, and on more than one occasion had provided his lunch and told him to hold onto her wages. As she said to him, very firmly, she worked to provide the icing on the cake, not the bread and butter of life.

She was a godsend. Now their accounts were firmly out of the red and Aidan had more work than one man could easily handle. If Jackie wouldn't take a step upward, and she said she wouldn't, then he needed to hire someone else to help with the workload. Whoever would have thought his little advertising firm would take off so well?

The phone rang again, breaking into his reverie. He'd worry about the need for more staff later. For now he'd answer the damned thing.

He picked up the instrument and enjoyed the feel of the soft, tactile handset under his fingers. He was pleased he'd followed Jackie's advice and gone for a reconditioned early 1950s one. It was fun and had so much more soul than a modern, hands-free piece of plastic. As he listened to the old-fashioned bell—no silly pop tunes or metallic notes—he wondered who Jackie had felt should be put through.

"Aidan, it's your father on the line," Jackie said in a worried voice. It made him wonder what tactics his father had tried on his assistant this time to try to make her tell tales. "He sounds sort of annoyed."

"Nothing new there then." Aidan began to tidy the mess known as his pencil box. Why on earth was there half a tin of mints and three vouchers, all out of date, for ten percent off at his local Italian restaurant amongst the pens, pencils and felt tips?

Jackie groaned and the noise reverberated down the line. "No and this time I've upset him good and proper because I said a five grand bribe was chicken feed, and I got that as a bonus each month. I suggested he throw in tassel swinging as an incentive."

She didn't get anything like the amount she'd teased his father with, but he knew that sort of talk would really piss his parent off.

"Mind you, he wasn't pleasant when I answered the call, and he's a lot less so now, than he was. Sorry, you'll no doubt get the flack, but he'd make a saint swear. You know sometimes I wish he'd show up here. Even if it was just so I could laugh at him. How he could have helped produce you, I have no idea. Are you sure your mum didn't play away or you were adopted?"

Aidan laughed as he reckoned she'd meant him to. "No such luck. I look like my grandpa on Dad's side. Put him through, Jacks, and then, sod it, we're going to shut up shop and have an early finish. We deserve it."

"Too right, and like I said, I'll have a man around tonight. Shugie's due back at eight. That'll give me time to, er, prepare."

She gave her smoky, dirty laugh. One that never ceased to amaze Aidan, as she was adamant the only thing she'd ever smoked was not nicotine, was illegal and that it was only once. She confessed she'd been sick as a dog, and from then on got her highs from music and dancing.

"Dinner," she added. "Oh, and dessert."

The inference in her voice lightened the black mood the information regarding the caller had given him.

"My father?" Aidan prompted, even though he'd rather have a root canal treatment than deal with the man.

"Shit, forgot about his arsiness still holding on. Do you want me to buzz in after two?" Jackie asked him.

Bless her. "Yeah, but make it five minutes or he'll not have vented his spleen. Either he'll be back on the line again, or take it out on mum long distance. After all, I don't have to listen properly. I can put him on loudspeaker and tidy up around him."

"Okay, good luck."

He didn't need Jackie's intervention this time. His father's demand for him to 'Give up that stupid perverted lifestyle you live, and come back here' he responded to with a flat no. After a few pithy swear words and a 'You'll never get anywhere without my backing' speech that Aidan knew word for word, his father issued a threat.

"I'll make sure you stop that crap. No son of mine is going to be a pervert. You tell those weirdoes to watch out. Either they get rid of you, or I'll get rid of them." The line went dead as he ended the call.

Aidan whistled. He had no illusions about his father. The old sod never issued idle threats, as several of his competitors had discovered. Never anything against the law, but Aidan wouldn't have been surprised to find out it was a close run thing. Jeff, the co-owner of Diomhair, would need to be warned to take care. It had occurred to him his father might already have meddled. There had been more than one occasion lately where suspicious activity had been discovered on and around the estate that belonged to Diomhair. In one instance it had endangered life, and they were all very alert these days.

Aidan frowned as he closed down his computer and locked up the desk drawers. There was no way he was going to let his father interfere with or upset his life, or that of his close friends. Never again would Aidan deny his needs and wants for the sake of an uneasy relationship with his parent. Not even if Hell froze over. Nor would he ever be at his father's beck and call and work for him. It had taken Aidan a lot of soul searching to decide he had to stand up to the domineering man and tell him he wasn't willing to compromise his lifestyle for the sake of his father's perceptions and preferences. Unfortunately, it seemed the elder Jefferies wasn't prepared to accept that.

Whatever anyone thought to the contrary, Aidan's desires as a Dom were as necessary to him as breathing. Not every day, and not in a whole lifestyle scenario, not anymore. But he was a Dom, and as such could not and would not be anything else. His parent demanding he stay away from all things even remotely connected with BDSM was a no go, and he'd said so.

His father had retaliated by sacking him from the company business, removing him from his will and effectively washing his hands of him. As he also refused to give Aidan references or salary in lieu of notice, at first, money had been tight. Only a lovely and unasked for loan from his godmother, along with the offer of a cottage she no longer used, had saved him from the dole queue.

Aidan had packed his bags, walked out of his company flat and never looked back. Within a year or so, by dint of hard work, two jobs and scrimping and saving, he'd repaid the loan and been flabbergasted when his godmother had gifted him the cottage.

"Saves a bit of inheritance tax," she'd told him with a grin.

Now after listening to his father ranting, he wondered how he'd stuck it all for so long. From the first flogger his father had 'discovered' hidden under Aidan's bed—who had given his parent that information? he wondered—to the threats to use it on him. Such as, 'I'll show you what for', blustering and threatening to show him what a 'real' whipping was like. His father was a bully. If it hadn't been for his mum, his gentle, wouldn't say boo to a goose let alone Murison Patterson Jefferies mum, Aidan would have left sooner. Eventually, though, his mum had urged him to leave.

"I will if you will," she'd said.

They both had. Leona Jefferies moved to Lanzarote to be close to her sister, then to live a happy and fulfilled life, and eventually get a rich Spanish boyfriend, and Aidan to Scotland. To also live a happy and fulfilled life, but until recently not anywhere approaching rich.

"Okay, are you all set?" Aidan asked Jackie as he locked his office door behind him. He took his jacket and bike helmet down from the cloak stand and helped Jackie into a bright, multi-colored fluorescent jacket that almost hurt his eyes. It clashed magnificently with her electric blue skirt and flowery Doc Martens.

"Yep. You okay? I didn't hear any shouting or the stapler hitting the wall."

"I didn't need to go that far. He worked himself up into an early temper and hung up. Thank goodness. I can't spare the energy to interact with him. It's much too exhausting. Anyway that'll be it for a few weeks until something or someone else rattles his cage." Aidan had no intention of worrying Jackie by sharing his father's threats unless he had to. "Right, let's be off."

"You're on." Her feather earrings stroked her shoulders and she flicked them away with impatience. "Damned things, I should know better."

* * * *

Every time he drove the ten minutes or so it took to ride his precious Ducati from one village to the next, Aidan realized over again how right he'd been to have his office away from the house. It gave him time to wind down and, in his mind, change from Aiden the ad-man to Aidan the whatever he fancied. Tonight he needed those few minutes of enjoyment that his bike brought him. The conversation with his father had rattled him more than he'd realized. By the time he turned the bike into his driveway, he was relaxed and ready for a chilled out evening.

His phone rang as he unlocked the front door. Aidan didn't think it would be his father, not yet. His way was to simmer for a few days, plot and plan then send in the big guns. Whatever or whoever they were.

Last time it had been Lynette. A pneumatic brunette who was supposed to be a lawyer, and a wannabe sub. He'd soon found out that, apart from the fake breasts, that was wrong on both other counts. She'd lit no spark of interest in Aidan whatsoever and in a fit of pique had revealed she was there on his father's behest. To blackmail him into, as she called it, turning normal or being taken to court.

Aidan had waved her goodbye instead.

He kicked the door shut behind him, dropped the bike and house keys in the ornate porcelain bowl on the side table and fished his mobile out of his jeans pocket. As ever it snagged. He swore under his breath, released it and answered the call. It was from Jeff, one of the owners of Diomhair, who sounded more than flustered.

"Shit and bugger, Ade, thank God I got you. I know you need an evening off, but you did say you had nothing planned. Shit, please don't now tell me you've got a hot date with a leggy blonde or whatever. Oh blimey, why does it happen like this? Jess and David are away overnight and, hells bells, Kath's gone into labor." Kath was his sub and partner, who was due to give birth to their twins, obviously somewhat earlier than anticipated. Jess was his sister and co-owner of Diomhair. David was her Dom and her husband. They were all people Aidan counted amongst his closest friends

"It wasn't supposed to happen yet. Fuck, she's due to go in at the weekend for a section," Jeff continued in a rush. His words tumbled over each other. "Two babies and all that, and her being little. Oh damn information overload and I'm babbling. Yes, pet, I won't be long." Aidan assumed that was for Kath, not him.

"Anyway, Ross isn't capable of leading wax, or knife play, not yet, and there's a potential sub booked a private session. She's been cleared and everything, but can you help? I really don't want to cancel if possible because she's said how worried she is. I reckon it's now or never, and God almighty she shouts sub. She's been to several group nights and now wants to take it a step further. Ross will be there as back-up, as will Connie Dores. Otherwise I'd have told her to reschedule." There was a strange keening noise from the phone.

"Hell. Look we have to go. I'm not up to delivering babies. Can you do it?"

Aidan assumed Jeff meant the session, not acting as a midwife. There was only one possible answer. "Of course, what time?"

"Seven." The phone went dead.

Poor Jeff, he sounded frazzled. Kath and he were happy and settled, with a wedding in the offing once, as Kath put it, her boobs didn't enter the room ten minutes before the rest of her. However, the imminent birth of his children seemed to have turned the steady, level-headed Dom into a gibbering idiot. *Poor bloke.*

Instead of steak and Shiraz, Aidan settled for salad and water. If he was showing a sub wax play, or any type of play for that matter, he didn't need the heavy stomach that steak would give him. He never ever drank and played so that didn't enter the equation. By six-thirty he was dressed in his favorite leather trousers and a black T-shirt, back on his bike and on his way toward Diomhair. Aidan remembered Jeff hadn't given him any information about the wannabe sub. No name or description. However, if Ross didn't know, all the details should be in the computer.

He guided the powerful bike around the potholes in the back drive of the castle. It was the most direct way for him to enter and shaved several miles off the distance he would cover if he used the more conventional route. Aidan sometimes thought that the upkeep of the track must be like the Forth Road Bridge painting cycle. A never-ending job to keep it up to scratch. Slowly he circled the castle to put the bike in the garage he habitually used. A red Honda was parked nearby and as he left the garage and locked it, Ross and Connie got out of the other vehicle. They weren't a couple yet, but Aidan had noticed how they gravitated toward each other whenever possible, and Connie deferred to Ross whenever they *were* together.

"Hey, you two, you're my back-up then?" He pulled the key to the castle's main door out of his pocket and dealt with the security alarm. Once inside he switched off the extra detectors that had been added over the last few weeks. Ever since Jeff had decided someone had entered the building via the secret passage built into the walls.

"Right-o, let's go in and get stuff sorted. Do we have any details regarding the potential sub?" Aidan asked them. "Name? Age? Sex?"

Ross shook his head. "I just got a frantic phone call to make sure I could still come and bring Connie with me. I tell you, man, the groans and swear words I could hear in the background were gruesome. I never knew Kath had such an extensive cussword vocabulary. I was impressed. Mind you, most of them seemed to involve cutting off Jeff in his prime. And making sure he never got her into the situation again. I just said sure and let them head off to be parents."

Aidan shrugged. The only annotation in the diary was *A. 7. Maybe sub? Wax or knife. Ross and Connie to assist.* No wonder Ross had baulked at taking charge. It was acknowledged that Aidan or Jeff were the best Doms for those scenes, although Aidan thought once Ross gained confidence, he'd give them a run for their money.

"Ah well, we'll know when she turns up. Okay, let's get sorted. I was told seven and it's quarter to."

It took scant minutes to make sure everything was as it should be and a further thirty to decide that whoever the wannabe—or it seemed now not so wannabe—sub was, she'd decided not to show.

Aidan thanked Ross and Connie for their attendance and offered them a dungeon to play in. To his amusement, they both blushed and shook their heads. With time on his hands, Aidan decided to spend some of it practicing his knife throwing. Not run-of-the-mill D/s play, but something he enjoyed. Especially when he imagined it was his father he had pinioned to the revolving circle of wood, with the knives landing close enough to make Murison Jefferies sweat. Aidan hadn't realized he had a malicious streak until that enjoyable scenario had flashed into his mind a few months earlier.

After he'd finished and cleaned his knives, he intended to have a sweaty session on the running machine in the tiny gym Jeff had had installed for his family and friends to use. Owing to pressure of work, and play of the nicest kind, Aidan had neglected it lately. He'd only just managed to snag the odd run here and there, and he missed the routine. A good spell on the treadmill and the punch bag would do him good.

He made a swift phone call to David, to apprise him of the situation and assure him there was no need to return to the club. Evidently they were on their way back, but would go straight to the hospital to see what was happening there, and text Aidan if there was any news.

Aidan nipped into the Dom's locker room, grabbed his sports bag and black running shorts and a T-shirt, which had lost the sleeves in a new washing machine/clueless male incident months before. It suited him fine for working out. In a much better frame of mind than he had been earlier, he headed to toward the gym. He'd change there and shower afterwards in the tiny locker room next door. With a much lighter heart, he whistled as he scrolled down the messages on his phone and listened to a call on his answer phone.

Chapter Two

Damn, blast and fuck. Someone had gotten the supposed timings all wrong. Deep inside Diomhair castle, Ailsa McLagan heard a tuneful whistle, glanced along the corridor in the direction from where it was coming and swore roundly. There was no way she could afford to be caught there. She took a deep breath and opened a door on her right. It led into a shoebox-sized cupboard with dusty shelves and not much else. Just as well. Taking care not to hit her elbow on the wall, she slid onto one of the shelves, and closed the door behind her, thankful to see a handle on the inside. She well remembered getting locked in the under stair cupboard at her gran's by accident, or goaded on by her cousin, it was a toss-up as to which was the reason. There hadn't been a handle on the inside. Gran just leaned hard on the door if she ever shut herself in. The four-year-old Ailsa wasn't heavy or strong enough to do that.

By the time someone had realized she was missing, she'd been in there a good ten minutes. The darkness hadn't bothered her. The thought of spiders had, and her screams had gotten louder and louder, until she was discovered. Then she was pulled out and to her annoyance had had her bottom smacked for disobeying her gran's edict to stay away from it. She'd never like corporal punishment, but after that, even a playful pat was enough for her to clench her teeth and her fists.

Dust tickled her nose as she remembered the ignominy of having her bum smacked in front of her cousin Sandra. To give Sandra her due, Sandra had tried to say it was her fault, but she'd been ignored. Ailsa had been scolded before on more than one occasion when she'd tried to go inside the cupboard. It held some strange fascination for her. Well up to then. Right up until her gran left the house for a smaller, compact bungalow more than twenty years later, Ailsa had never ventured near it again. Even when she'd helped Gran move, the cupboard remained in her 'oh no, not me' area.

Something tickled her cheek and she bit back a scream. It was a tendril of her hair that had fallen forward, not a spider. A noise outside made her even less inclined to open her mouth. Somehow she managed not to move—it was handy being pint sized—or sneeze as voices got louder.

"...a waste of time," a male voice said.

A deeper voice replied, but it came through the door as an indistinct rumble and Ailsa couldn't have sworn whether it was someone else there, or someone on the end of a speakerphone. Then there was silence. Ailsa counted to fifty and opened the door a crack. The corridor was empty. She eased herself down from the shelf and looked at the dust that coated her.

If anything would give away her presence, a trail of dust would, and she wasn't supposed to be found.

So much for good, clean undercover work. How many times had she wished she was back on the beat, policing a football match or shepherding drunken undergrads back to their lodgings? Well not many, she owned, but sometimes she wondered if she was right in the head. This job wasn't all glamorous parties and secret microphones. Most of it was standing in the freezing cold and waiting for something and you had no idea what for.

She wiped her shoes on the inside of her coat, held them in one hand, slipped her mucky socks into her pocket and walked quietly away in the opposite direction from where the voices had gone. Ailsa mentally smiled at her thoughts. Independently acting voices and no bodies to go with them?

God she hoped not, she wasn't a sci-fi or horror fan.

Stupidly she turned left not right and found herself in the gym.

And heard the whistling again.

It seemed someone was about, and she was going to be in big trouble. There wasn't even a desk to hide under like in all good movies, or a floor length curtain. The windows had fitted blinds. A treadmill, cross trainer and rowing machine didn't make good hiding places. Nor did the water cooler.

With a sigh deep enough to clear leaves from a footpath, Ailsa slipped her shoes back on, straightened her shoulders and faced the door.

The man who stopped dead in the doorway, mid whistle, was hot enough for her chin to drop, her eyes to widen and her body to tighten. Whoever said there was no such thing as instant lust was oh so very wrong. She might not subscribe to lacy thongs that got stuck up your arse like a cheese grater, but if she did, Ailsa reckoned they'd be wet and wrung out. As it was, her sensible, cotton, chain store knickers were damp under her thermals. Dark, soft, leather trousers and a black T-shirt were the clothes her wet dreams were made of.

He dropped the bag he was carrying, straightened then looked her up and down. "Well now, what have we here?"

Ailsa swallowed. How to reply to that and not be in trouble?

"Pet, answer me."

The tone sent shivers down her spine, and the hairs on her arms stood on end in sympathy. Ailsa gulped. Who on earth did he think she was? Pet? Should she woof or growl? If there was one thing she hated it was being called silly names like pet, or chick. She was a woman, not an animal.

"Pet, are you wanting a punishment? The mood I'm in I'll be happy to oblige. Surely you know the basic protocol?" There was no give in the harsh voice.

Well, no she didn't, not unless you counted what she'd read in books and that was all fantasy and fiction—wasn't it? She hadn't even ventured around the club part of the castle. Her time inside the place was too limited to explore unnecessarily.

"Hello, I'm Ailsa McLagan." *Dumb, Ailsa, now he can trace you.*

"Sir."

Eh? "Pardon?" *Oh fuck. Not a scooby. No way.* "No, I'm a miss. And you are?" *Apart from a prick? I thought Doms were… Oh actually, nope, oh double shit.* "Um, oh, sorry, er, Sir, well you see I just forgot where I was. I'm scared." Would he believe her?

"Really. Do you remember now?" It seemed sarcasm was his forte.

God, that voice. I could drown in it, sarcasm or not. Double dipped chocolate velvet and ohh shit, steel. Hard, hard steel. What do I do now? Come on, what would that dippy heroine from the last book you deleted from your eReader do? No not her, think of the other one. The one whose Sir made you wet. See, a Sir, oh, you ninny, Ailsa.

"Yes, I do, sorry, Sir. I got lost." She played the dumb blonde for all she was worth.

He gave her no idea if he'd fallen for the act or not. He just stared at her. And continued to stare.

Why doesn't he say or do something? It was enough to make a saint fidget, and Ailsa knew damn well she was no saint. At last, just as she was about to do her impersonation of a blubbering idiot, whatever it is, it w-wasn't me, dumb blonde routine, he nodded and tapped his hand on his thigh.

"You're late. This is the gym, not the main club room. How did you get in here?"

Okay so it looked like Mar Take No Prisoners, Sir was expecting someone. Who hopefully hadn't shown up? Maybe, just maybe, Ailsa thought, she could turn that to her advantage.

"I opened the door, and—"

"Don't get bratty." He stopped her mid-sentence. "Bratty subs, wannabe or not, get punished." His voice was level, and he showed no emotion. He just continued to look at her with his dark, unblinking gray eyes.

Sub? Bratty? Oh shit. Was he expecting a sub? Ailsa had a lump in her stomach. And for the life of her she didn't know if it was a hot 'Oh, my God, what next?' lump or an 'Oh, my God, not on your life' one.

"Oh sorry." *Shoot.* "Sir."

"Better. So let me ask again, how did you get inside?"

Ailsa opened her eyes wide and put on her best innocent expression. "I just walked through the door. I thought that was what I was supposed to do. I'm sorry if it wasn't. I'll just go then." She edged toward the door. "Excuse me."

"No." He stood immobile in the doorway, blocking her exit.

"I beg your pardon?" Even though her heartbeat sped up, Ailsa hoped her demeanor didn't show her agitation. After all, he had a good foot in height and several stone in weight to his favor. She might be nippy on her feet, but she had to get past him first.

"You came for a lesson, so a lesson you'll have. My father would be most disappointed if you missed out. I have to give him what he thinks he wants."

His father? What on earth is he talking about?

"I'm sorry if your father will be sorry, but what's that got to do with me?" Ailsa asked him. Had she slipped into a time warp? Was her boss playing tricks on her for not handing in her expenses on time? Why the hell had she left the beat? She could be safe behind a riot shield listening to rude chants about her sexuality now, or typing up yet another D and D report instead of wondering how to worm her way out of whatever she'd gotten into. Mind you, it did add credibility to her boss's belief of nefarious deeds being done.

Who was this bloke? It would be helpful to know his name. So she could tell her colleagues who the nutter was if she ever got away. Ailsa took a quick mental inventory. Tall, short dark hair, gray eyes, an arse to die for and abs... *Whoa, girl*, that *can't go into an identikit description.*

"You tell me," he said cryptically. "Right, let's move." He took her arm and swung her through the doorway after him. "So are we going for wax or knife?"

He was crazy. Surely even a Sir or Dom didn't pick up random women and ask them that? Then Ailsa remembered he'd said she was late. She didn't think he meant her as in her Ailsa McLagan, or she hoped he didn't, else she had slipped into a nightmare. Therefore it must be as she thought and he'd mistaken her for someone else. She'd best go along with it until she could make her getaway.

"Ohh, er, well, you see." She giggled. *Grief, I sound like a right idiot.* "I really don't know. I mean, should I?"

He stopped dead and as he was towing Ailsa along in his wake she bumped into him. All hard muscles and sinews, a body that she'd bet would look great in boardies and not much else.

Down, girl. He's too much everything for you. You need to get away, not stay.

"Oh, I so think you should." He turned and looked at her face, without releasing his grip on her arm. The voice was smooth, but no one could have mistaken the steely note of authority in it. "After all, why waste the evening, and your money? If you're worried I'm not Jeff, even he'll say I'm a better teacher in wax and knife play than he is."

What? Think here. "Then why was I booked with him?" Hopefully it was a good guess.

"Because I was busy. Now I'm not. Except with you. You have my whole attention."

That was what she was worried about.

Ailsa studied the guy from under her lashes. "What did you say your name was?" she asked him.

He flicked her chin then held it in one hand to lift her head up. Her neck cranked back as she was forced to gaze upward at an impossible angle.

"Well now, pet, all you need to know is between these walls, you call me Sir."

The inflexion in his voice, his intense gaze on her, with eyes that seemed to see into her soul, and the slight pressure on her chin made her heartbeat speed up. *Go on, admit it, you're curious. I know but what if I hate it and stuff? Well there's a get out clause isn't there? Shout red. That's what they do in the books. And the Doms try to persuade them different. Oh, sheesh, do I? Don't I?* Ailsa had a mental conversation with herself as she stood in front of the Dom. To agree would help her in more than one way. Both to get out of the castle without having to explain why she was there, and to satisfy her curiosity. If only she knew what his father had to do with it all. Was that someone she needed to check up on? Then she'd need to find out who this man was first.

"So, pet. What's it to be? Perhaps you want a little of each?" The hold on her chin tightened just enough to sting.

Ailsa swallowed. It was so hard to think when her mind was full of him. "I think maybe wax, Sir." After all, it was something that made her go all gooey inside when she read about it. "Yes, wax, please, Sir." Why did using the salutation sound so natural? His demeanor certainly helped but so did the knowledge of where she was. Little pinpricks of excitement bombarded her, and she metaphorically held her breath until he let go of her chin and nodded.

"Very well, pet. You're overdressed, but we'll sort that in a second. Assume the position." He crossed his arms over his chest and continued to stare at her without blinking. "You can do that?"

It took Ailsa all her concentration not to wriggle. *Overdressed? Sort it? Do it?*

"Waiting, pet."

Oh Lordy. She'd been so mesmerized by his look she'd forgotten what he'd asked of her. *Now come on, remember the books.* Ailsa dropped to her knees, not very gracefully. A slight run in with the car fender when her arms were full of groceries had left her with a swollen and bruised knee. She gasped as the tender skin made contact with the wooden floor.

"What's wrong?"

"The car fender and I had a coming together and my knee came off worse."

He frowned.

"First rules, pet. Open and honest. I asked you if you could assume the position. Your response should have been that due to an injury, it wasn't possible. Then we make our own rules."

Oh shoot, messed up already. I should know that. I've read enough books where that's stressed. She decided there was a dumb blonde moment needed.

"I'm excited, scared, flustered and nervous, Sir," Ailsa said in a quiet voice. It was true, even if she was overemphasizing everything. Never had so many different emotions vied to be uppermost in her. It was as if each one was on a pogo stick in her stomach and bouncing up and down as if their life depended on it. "I wanted to do as you asked, and I didn't think."

He put his hands under her arms and helped her to stand up. "I'm glad you wanted that, but you have to remember the rest. How can I be sure what we're doing is safe, sane and consensual if you aren't honest? That's the first thing anyone learns. It worries me that you forgot it."

She knew the rule. How on earth had she managed to screw up so badly so soon? Ailsa hoped to hell she'd be able to talk her way out of the situation. She didn't think her boss would be happy if she had to confess how she'd ballsed things up. And as for the rest of the team? The teasing she'd get there wasn't worth thinking about.

"I know, Sir, I'm sorry, it was an automatic reaction." She dipped her head and stared at the floor between them. Not only was it respect — she hoped — it also meant he wasn't staring into her eyes. He seemed to know exactly what was in her mind.

"Good in one way, very bad in another. If I were your Master, you wouldn't be able to sit down for a week after that silliness. How long have you been a sub?"

It was just the question she'd hoped he wouldn't ask.

Chapter Three

Aidan looked down at her bowed head. Her blonde curls teased the nape of her neck and covered her ears. Not the sort of woman he'd usually go for, so his father had slipped up there. Once he found out what his father was up to, Aidan had no qualms about nipping any budding relationships before they started. It had been a fair while since the last time he'd been in the line of fire and he wondered if this was the next round.

Previously there had never been any real emotions involved on either side, and Aidan had always been canny enough not to admit to either the women or his father that he knew what had been going on. Therefore, since the last time, he'd been waiting for another attack somehow.

The recent phone call confirmed what he thought. His father was on yet another mission to reform his son. Aidan hadn't thought the occasion would happen quite so soon. He'd bet his parent didn't know he'd sent a natural sub, though. She might be as innocent as they come, and he doubted she'd know a Shibari rope from a clothes line, but he'd seen the way she looked at him and her inclination to please.

How on earth had she been vetted and admitted to the club beforehand, though? That phone call had only occurred that day, and it had been several months since Aidan had received any other communication from his father. Something didn't add up. It wasn't like Ross to not check the door was secure when he left, but here she was inside the castle. Something stank.

Aidan knew he wasn't going to play with Ailsa that evening. He didn't know her, there was no one else around as back-up, and he wasn't setting himself or Diomhair up for any trouble. But he did intend to see what information he could get out of her. He didn't believe for one minute that she'd just wandered around looking for someone. To snoop, maybe.

The question was how far could he push her and still maintain the upper hand without being liable to any trumped up charges she or his father could manufacture?

"As you're unable to crawl, pet, we'll leave that for later." Her indrawn breath gave him some satisfaction. "Follow me. We need to talk."

He turned and walked down the corridor toward a large open area where people could gather to chat without waiting to see if she followed him or not. Behind him, he heard her shoes tapping over the parquet. That in itself told him something wasn't quite right. Any sub who played or socialized at Diomhair knew that their shoes were left in their locker unless specifically requested to be worn by their Dom. Jeff wouldn't make such a request when he was training.

Aidan walked toward a large, soft armchair with a footstool next to it. In the later part of her pregnancy,

Kath had sat on it rather than on the floor next to Jeff when they were together, and watched a scene or chatted to friends. It seemed the obvious choice now. Aidan pointed at it, amused rather than irritated when her eyes flashed before she moved forward.

"You're learning, pet. I'm going to sit on this seat. Sit on that stool and face me. Once you're seated, bow your head and put your hands on my knees." Aidan sat down and watched as she did as he asked. The heat of her palms traveled through his trousers and warmed his skin. Almost like a tattoo, he thought, as he imagined her handprint embossed on his leg. The simple gestures gave him a warmth inside himself that he hadn't experienced for so long he'd forgotten how arousing it was.

"Such a good pet. So if I tell you to strip and stretch out on that table over there, you will of course do it."

Her head came up so fast it was a wonder she didn't pull a muscle in her neck.

"Um, what was it we needed to discuss about safe words and stuff?"

Ailsa sounded both hesitant and, he reckoned, not uninterested. He'd wondered when she'd think of that. He waited just long enough for her to let her head fall a little, then spoke.

"You tell me."

Her head jerked up once more and her eyes were wide as she stared at him. "I don't know what you mean, Sir."

He wasn't letting her get away with that. "Don't lie, pet. You know and you understand. Blonde hair and blue eyes don't spell silly or bimbo to me. You can't disguise the intelligence in your eyes, however much you try. So do us both the courtesy of not attempting to. Now, it's honesty time, or goodbye time. Cut the crap and tell the truth." He ended on a harsh note that grated, even on him. "What the hell is going on here?"

She swallowed and as Aidan watched her, a soft sheen of perspiration began to cover the fine hair of her arms. Evidently his suspicions of something untoward were correct.

"If you've been playing with Jeff, then you'd have asked me about safe words ages ago," he said emphatically. "Asked me if I truly knew what I was doing, and why I hadn't checked what you knew and understood."

"I was scared."

Aidan shook his head. "Balls. I think, Miss, whoever you are, there's a nice dungeon down the corridor where a little punishment play might help you to clear your mind and be honest."

She gasped and lost every bit of color she had. "Red, Red, and Red. I'm sorry. But I came to learn more about wax play, not to be flogged or whatever. Perhaps I'd best leave now." She lifted her hands from Aidan's knees and stood up.

"Sit down, pet." Aidan rapped the words out and was surprised when she responded instantly and did as he demanded, even to dipping her head and replacing her hands on his knees. "Thank you." He softened his tone. "So you know your safe swords?"

"Yes, Sir." Her voice was low.

Aidan stared at the tousled curls that looked as if they were a devil to tame, and decided he loved short, blonde, curly hair. Trying to get to the bottom of the mystery was going to be fun. As long as it didn't impact badly on the club.

"They are?"

"Red, stop, and you may come back to it later. Yellow, stop and talk, and green is okay… Er, Sir."

Aidan was glad she couldn't see his face. He was sure the amusement on it would send her away in a huff, and that was the last thing he wanted. She sounded like a flustered kitten, if there was such a thing. Or should that be a prickly cat? One thing was for sure. She *was* flustered and that had to be good. It might enable him to get some information from her. He intended to push her as far as he could without putting himself up to all sorts of accusations. For one fleeting moment he wished Ross and Connie were around so he could play with her. However, something told him that whatever had occurred previously, if anything, she was nowhere ready to play at the level she was supposed to be expecting.

"You're green with wax?" Why did he think that statement should really be green *as* grass? "And look at me now before you answer."

Aidan waited as she slowly lifted her head and stared at him. He watched the play of the muscles in her throat as she swallowed. His cock hardened. Why on earth something like a swallow should do that, he had no idea, but it seemed it did. Her skin rippled as she swallowed again, and Aidan tingled with tension.

Ailsa straightened her spine and Aidan could sense her determination.

"Yes, Sir."

It was his turn to sigh with relief, even though he wouldn't be able to follow through.

"Then one day we will."

"What?"

"We don't play here without a Dungeon Master," Aidan said. "As you were late, our Dungeon Master left. So, nothing doing tonight. Except maybe we talk."

He'd never understood the expression 'her face fell' until then. It was somewhat satisfying to know she was as disappointed as he was.

"Yes, Sir, but seriously. I'm so sorry I was late. I should have let you know, but it sounds so lame."

"What does?"

She grinned. The smile lit up her eyes, and the skin at the corners crinkled. "Three stray sheep and no way to get by."

"You're right, it does sound lame. However, knowing the area, I won't dismiss that excuse without a thought. I've been held up by an errant pheasant and his harem more than once." Aidan watched her closely and saw the way she let her breath out in relief. So it was an excuse? The rush of disappointment that filled him surely outweighed the occasion? "While I remember, where's your transport?"

She blinked and stared at him. He could almost see the cogs in her mind whirring.

"In a lay-by not far from the gate. That's part of the sheep scenario. I decided it would be quicker to jog through the grounds, rather than try to get past them."

She's lying. Oh I don't doubt the car or whatever is where she says it is, but as for the rest? Not true. Now all he had to do was fathom out what the hell she was playing at. Aidan didn't doubt for a moment it would be like trying to prize a razor clam open without getting scratched.

"And was it worth it?"

His phone buzzed, and Aidan cussed under his breath. Until he saw who was ringing.

"It's us." Ross' voice came clear over the line. "We changed our mind. Can we come and play?"

Aidan grinned. What a perfect answer. "Sure, if you'll help me out first. We seem to have a sub who has lost her way. Now she's found and ready to play. A nice little wax scene, I think."

He saw her face pale and she bit her lip. Her shoulders shook, and he guessed it took all of her determination not to run.

Gotcha, Miss. Now let's see what you're really here for.

Alisa kept her head down and dug her nails into the palms of her hands. Now if only he'd go to the door and let whomever it was inside, maybe she'd get out with her story unchallenged again.

I don't want to. I need to see if these tingles and shivers translate into something I like. Well, you don't always get what you want in this life so tough. Work comes first. And the secrecy of the job is paramount. Get out if you can.

Aidan walked to the wall and pressed something on a keypad she hadn't noticed. So much for thinking she'd get out. Now it didn't seem like a possibility, Ailsa relaxed. Damn it, she'd play and see if her suspicions about how good it could be were correct. Mind you, wax? That was something she couldn't decide if it was nightmares or dreams. It might make her wet when she read about it, but reading and reality were poles apart. However, it seemed she might be about to find out.

Voices from outside the room warned her they were soon going to be joined by others.

"Sir?"

Aidan turned and looked at her, with one eyebrow raised in query. "Yes?"

"I can color out?"

The look he gave her shriveled her insides.

"If you have to ask me that now, I'm somewhat concerned," Aidan said in such a flat tone her pussy muscles contracted. A turn-on it was not.

"Um, Sir…"

He didn't say a word just continued to look at her in a disinterested manner.

Ailsa lost her temper. She might be blonde and dizzy-looking, but her mum had been a red-haired hothead and Ailsa had inherited the temper, if not the looks. She forgot why she was in the castle, what her remit was, and spoke as a potential sub, not an undercover policewoman.

"Look, Sir." It wasn't said in a respectful tone. "If you're a bloody Dom then act like one. I'm shit scared, you're not Jeff, and Jess, who is an old school friend, has never mentioned you. For all I know, you could be an imposter, and just a wannabe Dom who has no Dom cred whatsoever." She'd forgotten it wasn't her he—or Jeff—had expected. "I have no idea why you're here, or even if anyone knows of you or can vouch for you. You could be a perv, an ax murderer or…"

Aidan let out a crack of laughter.

"So I could."

Ailsa accepted she was projecting her worries and trying to get rid of the sickness inside and replace it with excited anticipation instead. But there was more than a kernel of truth in her words. She stamped her foot in annoyance and ignored the way he firmed his lips and narrowed his eyes. Tough if he didn't like it, it was how she felt. How *did* she know? "How do I know?"

He inclined his head and clapped his hands slowly. The noise was loud in the quiet room. Each clap resonated deep inside her, and echoed the thud of her heart.

"At last. Real, honest emotion. Well, pet. You don't know, do you? I can say what I want." He paused. "Just as you can."

Ailsa bit her lip, as those words brought her back to her predicament with a jolt. She was lying, and had no way of sorting it any time soon.

"So, it all boils down to this," Aidan said to her. "Are you willing to trust me, and I you?"

The door opened before Ailsa could formulate an answer, and two people entered. She looked up, and swore under her breath. One of them was very well known to her. She glared at the person in question, who after one brief, startled glance looked away.

"Ross, Connie, this is Ailsa. Ailsa, you will address Ross as Sir. Connie is a sub, who will help you get ready. If you want to proceed?"

Ailsa nodded. His voice was all Dom and sent shivers down her spine. If he'd told her to roll on the floor, she'd be hard pressed not to. Something in the tone shouted 'obey or else'. She couldn't really do anything but, and apart from which, she wanted to know what the kiss of wax on her skin was really like. She gathered it was so different from accidentally dripping ordinary wax onto yourself. That was an 'ouch, swear, scratch it off and run your hand or whatever under the tap' moment. Wax play, according to the books she'd read, was the opposite. If this was her chance to try it, then Ailsa decided she would.

"I do. Sir, thank you."

Aidan smiled. This time it reached his eyes. The approval on his face unclenched her pussy muscles and let her juices gather.

"Off you go, and listen to Connie. Shower and no lotions, please. And no flowing laces, ribbons or loose ends. If you didn't bring anything suitable, Connie will find you something."

"Yes, Sir." *Thank goodness. I don't think boots and a camouflage jacket is what he means as suitable.* She followed Connie out of the room.

No sooner had the door shut behind them than Ailsa grabbed Connie's arm.

"What the fuck?" Ailsa glared at the other woman. Connie shook her head in warning.

"Not here." Connie mouthed the words. She raised her voice. "I'll keep you right, don't worry. Look, this is the subs' changing room. Feel free to ask questions as we change."

Ailsa gathered that Connie meant the changing room was private, and no one could overhear them there. She followed her inside a warm and cozy room, which held settees and floor to ceiling cupboards and mirrors.

"Showers and stuff through there." Connie waved toward a door at the rear of the room. "Any locker with a key in it is available for use. If you want to keep the same one, you arrange it with admin. We've got around fifteen minutes, and, ma'am, what the fuck are you doing here?"

Ailsa turned and stared, narrow-eyed, at the policewoman who stood next to her. The last time she'd seen Connie Dores, she'd worked under Ailsa as they had removed a child from a potentially dangerous situation, not long before Ailsa had been seconded to her present unit. Now here she was, and the one person who could blow Ailsa's cover sky high. So did she try to brazen it out or admit why she was there? Ailsa had to assume Connie was there for pleasure, not work. She hadn't missed the way Connie had interacted with Aidan or the other man.

Although she would have hoped the relevant information would have been shared to her if any other police departments were interested in Diomhair, Ailsa wasn't convinced it would necessarily have been the case. There had been plenty of cock-ups, and lack of information sharing over the last few years, for it not to be a reasonable assumption.

"The same as you, I imagine." Ailsa strove to keep her voice level. "Learning about subbing. And here I'm Ailsa, and don't mention work outside this room."

Connie opened a cupboard and took out some clothing and a towel.

"With respect, Ailsa, you're no more a sub than I'm a police inspector. Your demeanor screams boss. But as long as you're not here to threaten me, or my friends, I'll keep my mouth shut about how we know each other. Why are you here?"

She was like a terrier with a rat.

"As I said, deciding if I can sub. And finding out what I like." All of a sudden Ailsa realized that was true. Okay, her job was paramount, but the more she saw and heard, the more she wanted — no needed — to discover what was for her. "Look, Connie, I'll be honest." *Or as honest as I dare.* "Your secret, if that's what it is, is safe with me. If none of you are doing anything wrong, why would I be here to threaten you?"

Connie didn't say anything, then, slowly, she shrugged. "Because something screwy is going on. Nothing to do with the Doms or subs as far as I know. And it's not up to me to say any more. But maybe, once you're ensconced more comfortably, mind you if you go for a flogging maybe comfortably is not the word, you'll find out."

So it seemed Connie wasn't convinced but would keep her counsel for a while.

"And before you ask," Connie said. "I'm here because I *am* a sub, and hopefully Ross will be my Dom. He had a bad session with some eejit called Arperony... Holy hell, are you here because of her?"

The name meant nothing. Ailsa smiled. "Not unless she's who I have to show I can sub. So I need to shower?"

Connie looked at the clock. "Yep and fast. Do you have suitable clothing?"

Ailsa shook her head. "Only what I'm wearing."

Connie gave her a quick encompassing glance. "No, here, this will do for now." She handed two tiny garments to Ailsa who took them and looked at them doubtfully. Once on they wouldn't leave much to the imagination.

"God almighty, this doesn't leave me much covered. Ah, well, in for a penny..."

Connie snickered. Evidently Ailsa's outburst had worked in her favor.

"Okay, I'll go with what you say for now, but..."

Connie didn't finish her sentence. Ailsa decided to meet her halfway.

"As long as I'm not endangering you or your friends. If I ever think that, I'll tell you. Fair enough?"

"It will have to be, I guess. Now, please shower, dry and dress. No bra, just the top and skirt."

"And pants," Ailsa said in a voice that didn't encourage arguments. "That's non-negotiable." Even if they were department store finest. Her nice silky Janet Reger underwear wasn't worn on a stake-out.

"Whatever. You can argue the toss over that with Aidan. Just get a move on. I don't want my arse paddled because of you."

So he's called Aidan. Nice name, it suits him. Ailsa thought about the man as she did as she was asked. Was she going to see what transpired or would she wuss out? If she did she could kiss goodbye to any chance of getting to know him as well as getting inside Diomhair legitimately.

As she thought, the emerald green, thin-strapped top barely covered her breasts, and the darker hued skirt should be called a scarf, or a pelmet. A narrow one. However, she reckoned she had best not protest.

"Um, will I do?" she asked Connie, who had changed into a tiny red leather dress that clung lovingly to her curves.

Connie looked her up and down. "Turn round."

Ailsa did as she'd been asked.

"I guess." Connie didn't sound too sure.

Ailsa spun back again. "What do you mean you guess?"

"Well, Ma...er, Ailsa, with due respect. A sub doesn't usually look as if she's going to have her wisdom teeth pulled out with pliers. Unless she knows she's due punishment, which I guess you're not. You look about as comfortable as a Ranger fan in the Celtic stand at Celtic Park." Connie used a worst case football match scenario for comparison. "And you wonder why I have my reservations."

Put like that, Ailsa didn't.

Ailsa shrugged and bit her lip. "Okay, what I know could be written on a pin head and there'd still be space for the alphabet. All my knowledge is from hot erotic romances. So tell me what I need to know."

Five minutes later, her head was reeling and she was damned sure she wouldn't remember half of what Connie had told her. The one thing she did remember was respect and honesty. Red, yellow and green traffic lights for what happened, and if in doubt, tack Sir onto every sentence.

"Honestly, safety is taken very seriously here. SSC is the mantra, and everyone, Dom and sub alike, is vetted and vetted again," Connie told Ailsa as she tied her hair into a tight bun.

That was where Ailsa could call them out if she wanted to. However, she reasoned uneasily, that was her fault, not theirs.

"We're all very friendly and Doms or subs are open to chat and answer questions," Connie said as Ailsa followed her out of the room and along the corridor. "Well, Doms in the context of if you have permission. You'll soon learn all the rules and regs if you want to. It's a fantastic place. If you do decide to play, whatever way, then you'll soon learn that."

Ailsa had her doubts. If she did decide to play, she reckoned her inexperience would call her out, and there would be hell to pay. But she might as well see how far she could get and discover what she liked before that time was on her. Then when she was back on the beat on a Saturday afternoon, dodging spit and post-match sick, she could remember what might have been.

Chapter Four

"Something's fishy." Aidan checked his wax and equipment was as it should be, took off his shirt and put it into a tall, narrow cupboard in the corner of the room. He wasn't going to change into fresh leathers, not now, but clean, tight, midnight blue denims should work. Why he'd switched, he had no idea. To stave off disappointment maybe? Whoever Ailsa was, he thought his attire would be the last thing she'd worry about. "Either she's not who she says she is, or someone sure hasn't gone over the basics properly. I pushed as far as I could without going over the limits, and she just couldn't make up her mind how to play it. I do think she's a sub, but she doesn't know it. But is she the sub Jeff was expecting? That's the question. She just doesn't fit what I'd expect of someone Jeff's training."

"What?" Ross said, as he followed Aidan's example, clothes wise, and double-checked the equipment with Aidan. Surprise tinged his tone. "If she's not who Jeff was expecting, who the hell is she and how did she get in here?"

"That's what I want to find out." Aidan opened a cupboard and got out some cloths and a fire blanket. "She says she wants wax play, so I'll give her that. Mind you, there are a few more forms for her to fill in first."

"There are?"

Ross sounded surprised, which Aidan could understand.

"There are now, or there will be in three minutes. If they get in here before I'm back, go over the protocol or something please. I'm off to be creative with the printer." He left the room at a run and within a few seconds was typing on the computer.

Three minutes later, Aidan was satisfied. The forms might not be drawn up by a lawyer, but if she signed them she'd have no reason to say she was forced or did anything against her own free will. It may well be overkill, but Aidan knew the benefit of leaving nothing to chance.

He was back in his chosen dungeon before Connie and Ailsa reappeared.

Aidan subjected Ailsa to a thorough inspection. Her eyes flashed, just once, before she looked toward the floor. In the tiny skirt and top she had on, she looked about as comfortable as his mum at a teen pop concert, or the proverbial nun in a whorehouse. He'd love to be able to read her thoughts.

"Well, pet? Ready?"

Ailsa lifted her head and he watched the skin across her ripple and tighten, as she swallowed before she blinked and cleared her throat.

"Yes, Sir." Ailsa ran her hands over the material that clung to her hips and tugged on the hem. Aidan hid his smile. He wondered what she'd say if he told her to take it off? He rather thought if he valued his balls,

Dom/sub or not, he wouldn't make any demand along those lines in a hurry. One day, though, he'd so love to see her bare and decorated with his waxy patterns. For now he'd be satisfied to see if she accepted his ministrations or cried red and ran.

"Then shall we start?" He didn't miss the way she looked at the table where he'd set his candles, and her eyes widened.

"Ye…es, Sir. What happens?"

Beside her, Connie stiffened and stifled a gasp. Aidan hid his grin once more. This was going to be fun.

"Firstly we'll run through the safety procedure, then you sign the disclaimer and we'll get started."

Competently he checked that she knew what she was to expect, made sure she read the new contract he'd worked out not long before, signed it, and watched as both he and Ross countersigned.

"I work in stages," he said as he took her hand and led her to a long waist-high bed, with the head higher than the base. "Stretch out on your back, and put your wrists and ankles next to the ties."

Ailsa stopped walking and he looked down at her. "What's wrong?"

She shook her head and the cluster of blonde curls swung around her skull like tight waves. "I'm calling red. No ties." She tugged on his hand, and Aidan held on tighter.

"Steady, pet. Now tell me what's wrong." He put his hand under her chin and tilted her head so she looked at him face on.

"No ties. I can't."

"So why isn't that on your list of hard limits?" She didn't answer and Aidan continued. "It's for your safety, pet. Otherwise if you rear up or jerk suddenly it could cause an accident. Wax is hot, and if it isn't used appropriately, it could burn or scar you. I want you to have the burn in a good way, feel the sting, embrace the pain and see the evidence on your skin. However, it isn't my intention to leave a lasting reminder. Do you understand?"

She was as pale as the lace curtain that used to hang at his granny's window, and she swayed a little, just like they had in the breeze. Aidan held her chin tight and used his other hand to rhythmically stroke her back from the nape of her neck to the base of her spine. He didn't speak, glad that Ross had summoned Connie to his side without a word, and the sub was sitting quietly at Ross' feet.

Under his hand, Ailsa shivered.

"Well? I do expect an answer, pet, even if it's just no, Sir."

"I understand your reasoning, but I'm not sure I can do it. And as for hard limits, I, er, haven't really thought of them."

Ross cleared his throat, and Aidan sent him a warning look. He saw 'Warning, not the sub you expected' written in big imaginary letters over Ailsa's head. Obviously Ross saw the same thing.

"Well, you need to. For now we'll just say, if you want to continue, for your own well-being, you need to be unable to move and perhaps cause yourself an injury. And before you argue…"

Ailsa shut her mouth.

"Good girl. Before you argue, I am not interested what happens elsewhere. This is how we do it here. So restraints or go." Aidan spoke in a no nonsense, 'that's my decision and you can like it or lump it' manner. He watched her closely, sensing her inner struggle. He could almost see her thoughts flow out of her.

Eventually, just as Aidan thought he might have to prompt her, Ailsa gave a long sigh, and looked up at him.

"I can cry red and it stops?"

"Immediately."

She bit her lip. "Then, okay, yes, I'll try."

Talk about sounding as if she's doing me a favor. Maybe it's as well she's not a true sub. She'd not last long.

He raised one eyebrow and she blushed.

"Sir."

The color flowed upward from her chest, and it did make Aidan think about how far down her body it started. One day he hoped he'd find out.

Hold it, I'm getting a hell of a lot too interested in someone who might be working for Dad. Pull back before I get burned, and not with the candle wax either. However, Aidan knew fine well he was going to ignore his own advice and see what transpired.

Aidan stood back and let her make her own way to the bed. She needed to know this was all her own doing. That it was her choice and what *she* wanted, not what she thought someone else wanted for her.

Ailsa stood on tiptoe and scrambled onto the hard mattress. It was set at a height for the Dom to work easily and gave no quarter to a five-foot-not-much-else sub. She used one hand to tug at the hem of her skirt once more. Aidan got a very brief glance of something red and cotton, before she stretched out — not very elegantly — on the bed. All of a sudden, plain red cotton held a fascination for him. He had to admit elegance and holding your clothes where you wanted them didn't go hand in hand.

Ailsa wriggled and pulled her top over her middle, before she put her hands and feet where Aidan had directed. He chose to ignore her unease. After all, he had reiterated the need to vocalize and cry red if necessary. Instead he studied her face until she looked away. Aidan tugged on one blonde curl of hair.

"Look at me." To his pleasure, she did so immediately. "Color, pet?"

Alisa ran her tongue over her lips. Such a small and, he reckoned to her, unconsciously sexy and arousing action. To him it was cock-twitching, dick-hardening, cum-inducing, out-and-out eroticism. His skin tingled, and the hairs on his arms stood on edge.

"Green, Sir."

He nodded, and leaned toward her to whisper in her ear, "You can red at any time. If you're worried, cry yellow. Remember, you're in charge."

Her eyes opened wide and the blue irises seemed to grow even bigger.

"Me?"

Yeah, she really does know jack shit. Aidan bit back the impatient retort he felt like giving. "You. You can make me stop at any time. Understand?" He waited until she replied in the affirmative. "Now, as this is really only a taster, I'll be gentle and talk you through it. Ross and Connie will be in the room, for extra protection for both of us."

Alisa began to shake her head.

Aidan put his hand on her cheek. "Yes. We do not play without back-up. Believe me, once I start you'll be too absorbed in the experience to know if the cast of every West End musical performed in front of you."

Ailsa gave a shaky laugh. "Now that would depend who was saying 'no one puts Baby in a corner'."

She took a very deep breath. Her chest swelled and Aidan wondered if her breasts would pop over the top of the vest. Connie had interpreted his demands to the letter and the vest was incredibly low and tight.

He patted Ailsa's cheek then moved down to the foot of the bed and fastened her ankles.

"You know you'd enjoy this a lot more if you took your top off," he said in a throwaway manner. As if it didn't matter in the slightest to him what she replied. "To experience the sting properly, you don't want material in the way. I may be good, but even I need a canvas of skin to play with to do the designs justice." After he checked he had the tension of the ties correct, he walked back toward the head of the bed, and looked directly into her eyes.

"Apart from which, candle wax is a sod to get off linen."

She chuckled. If he were fanciful, he would have sworn the blue irises darkened and sparkled.

"You gonna charge me the dry cleaning bill?"

Aidan grinned. She might be worried, her skin might be covered in perspiration and her lips red where she'd chewed at them, but she still had a sense of humor.

"I will do if you want. However, it would be easier just to take your top off."

"Or roll the straps down and the bottom up?"

"Or that. But still not as good as giving me the space to be creative on."

Out of the corner of his eye, Aidan saw Ross speak to Connie, who moved to the back of the room. Ross stood a few feet behind Ailsa. Close enough to intervene if necessary. Far enough away not to interfere between Dom and sub when all was well.

"I'm not sure I can go that far, Sir. Not yet." Not ever, her tone implied.

Aidan decided to leave the status quo as it was. "Then straps down and bottom rolled up to where you feel comfortable." Maybe she wasn't one of the topless and don't care brigade on the beach. Or maybe it was the fact that the small dungeon had an intimate feel to it, whereas a wide sandy beach was anonymous. Whatever, Aidan decided if they didn't move on, he'd waste his wax, and still be negotiating at midnight.

"Now, pet." He might as well let her know he was the Dom, and he was ready to move.

It worked. She sat up and carefully worked the straps over her shoulders and tucked them under her arms, before rolling the bottom of the top upwards and tucking it under her breasts. Then without any prompting, she resumed the prone position from before and put her wrists by the ties, ready for them.

Aidan didn't waste any more time, and fastened her as he wanted. "Remember it's up to you to tell me if you're uncomfortable. I can see signs, but I'm not a mind reader. Ross will be just behind you, and Connie will be in the room but out of the way."

He rolled the table on which he'd put what he needed nearer and took up the first candle.

"Look at me, pet. Remember to breathe and absorb the sting. Feel the heat, imagine how beautiful you'll look with a wax tattoo."

He held her gaze and carefully lifted the steadily burning candle high, before tilting it. Gradually, the wax slid down the taper. Gently the first drop began to fall, like a raindrop caught in slow motion, down toward Ailsa.

Before it hit, the next droplet formed and fell, and Aidan moved the candle to direct the flow.

The first wax touched.

Chapter Five

Ailsa couldn't take her eyes off the tiny teardrop shaped orb of molten wax as it fell toward her. It was all well and good being told to regulate your breathing, absorb the pain and breathe through it, but it didn't help at all when you had no idea what it all meant. Why hadn't she fessed up and said she wasn't the sub?

Because that would have dropped her even deeper in the mire and he might have been the one to say red.

The wax hit her chest and she gasped, made a noise between a sob and a scream and stifled the swear words that came to mind. The sting wasn't a sting. It was pain. Red hot radiating pain that filled her, and made her breath come in short, sharp pants, and caused her to pull at her restraints.

Her tongue felt like cotton wool, which filled her mouth and made it dry and unusable. It was hard to clamp down on the panic she felt. How could she shout red when her voice wouldn't work? Even the fact that Aidan was staring at her intently didn't help.

He said he could read her, damn it, so why wasn't he stopping?

It was like something out of a horror film as the next drop of wax, and the next got closer and closer to her body, and hit.

Onto the swell of her breasts, one by one and close to each other. The sting struck, the pain began… Ailsa coughed. "Ahhh, ohh r…" She stopped speaking. The pain was different. Oh it stung, but the sting was like someone was trailing their finger over her skin, creating tiny pulses of pleasure.

Aidan straightened the candle up so the wax gathered in the shallow dip by the wick.

"Color?"

His voice wasn't steady and that tiny hint of vulnerability resonated with Ailsa.

"Green, oh my, argh." She was babbling but didn't give a damn. "More please. Take my top off." She knew without a shadow of a doubt she wanted to see what he would achieve without having to try to miss the strip of cloth that covered her breasts. "Really, Sir, green. I want to feel it all. You were right, the pain isn't an ouchie pain, it's an 'I want to feel more' pain. Green."

Would he do as she wanted? How on earth could he, without untying her and spoiling the moment?

Three seconds later, Ailsa realized she shouldn't have worried. After all he was a Dom and probably used to subs changing their minds like they changed their knickers. Aidan nodded, put the candle down in a safety holder on the table, and lifted a wicked-looking knife from the table. The blade was a good nine inches long, with a serrated edge and a sharp point and the handle was thick and indented for fingers and thumbs, to enable the user to clasp it safely.

It was one thing to tell yourself that he would be more than competent when he used it, another not to find your heart beating faster when the tip slid almost lazily across your skin and the point lifted the wax that clung there. Aidan flicked the cold pieces away like he was brushing crumbs from a tablecloth. Then he slid the blade of the knife under her top between her breasts and pushed upward. The material parted as if it was held together by a thread, not a tight-knit weave, and slid over her sensitive breasts and nipples to allow cool air to caress them like a lover's kiss. Aidan smiled and rested the cold flat of the blade over her heart and moved it carefully over her skin.

"One day, I'll scribe you."

He said the words so quietly that Ailsa thought he was talking to himself.

"Ready to be decorated, pet?"

No more mention of scribing? Ailsa wasn't sure whether to be pleased or disappointed. Mind you, her idea as to what it meant was somewhat hazy. Scratches that didn't last? She made a mental note to research it. *Hold on, woman, learn to accept and like one thing at once. Walk, don't run.* Aidan cleared his throat, and Ailsa realized she hadn't answered him.

"Oh, yes, Sir." She regulated her breathing, a lot happier now she knew what to expect, and relaxed into the hard mattress as best as she could. How she wished her head was raised a little so she could see better.

Was he a mind reader? Aidan replaced the knife in its cover and bent to reach under the bed. With a whirring noise, the top third tilted a little, just enough for Ailsa to be able to look down her body. Then he stood back, picked up two candles and held one in each hand.

He didn't speak again, but began to rotate and move his hands. It was mesmerizing to watch as he twisted and turned them and wax slid and slipped down the length of their candles. Tiny granules formed and twisted and almost shimmered as they spiraled down toward her skin.

When the first one hit, Ailsa stopped thinking and let her senses fill her instead. The sting, the tug on her heart, the way her inner muscles tightened and her pussy throbbed, all morphed into one hazy, arousal-filled sensation of pleasure.

With each new arc of wax, somewhere else began to sting and sing. Aidan knew what he was doing, and created a web of wax to decorate her skin. Nothing formal but a beautiful intricate design that any abstract artist would be proud of. Something as good as an old master by a new Master. That thought would have made her snigger except she didn't want to miss one second of what was happening.

Then, suddenly it was over. Aidan put down the candles, untied her and wrapped the blanket Ross had handed him around her, without removing the wax.

Ailsa began to shake, and burst into tears. He cuddled her close and stroked her hair.

"Shhh, let it out, it's normal and natural. There, there." He held her close and whispered nonsensical words until she quieted.

Ailsa sniffed and looked around. "Can I have a tissue, please?"

Connie handed her one and she whispered her thanks. Her voice didn't seem to belong to her. None of her did. It was strange and disquieting.

She wondered what happened next. After all she was still coated in wax, half naked and in a room with virtual strangers. For the first time she saw the sense in having more than one person around. As long as they weren't all ax murderers.

After all, what did she know about any of them? Not a lot, not even about Jess, who after all could have changed considerably since school. And Connie might be a policewoman, but that wouldn't negate being a drug dealer or one of the aforementioned ax murderers.

Aidan pinched her cheek. "I can see your mind's back in gear, working overtime adding two and two and making seventeen. Just think how lucky you've been. An awesome play session with a fantastic Dom."

He rolled his eyes and she gave a half giggle. One thing was certain. He was able to make fun of himself.

"No one bugging you for answers to questions you know fine well you need to answer, and amazing aftercare. About which…" He stood up and carried her back on the table and set her down on the mattress. "Lie back." Once she did so he opened the blanket.

Ailsa experienced the horrible sensation of being naked and vulnerable.

"Time to lift the wax. Do you need fastening?"

"No, I'm fine." He raised one eyebrow and Ailsa realized she'd forgotten to add his title. She was too drained to care. To her intense relief he didn't comment or pull her up. He took up the knife once more.

"I'm lifting the wax with this. Hold still because otherwise there is the chance I might nick you."

The word nick conjured up a very different picture in Ailsa's mind. Handcuffs and…

Stop it. Concentrate on not getting cut.

Within a few minutes all the wax had gone and Aidan wrapped her in the blanket once more and lifted her into his arms before sitting in a comfortable armchair. Across the room Ross was holding Connie, and Ailsa discovered she had no idea what the couple had done, if anything. It was so unlike her to become so absorbed with one thing she was oblivious to everything else that it brought her up with a start. Not the way for an undercover policewoman to behave, even if there were extenuating circumstances. She was going to have to pull back and think things over. Ailsa gave herself the luxury of being held for a few moments. It was bliss to revel in Aidan's soft breath on her skin, the way he held her tight, but not uncomfortably so, and the way he nuzzled her head and occasionally stroked her back over the blanket.

As much as she could have stayed like that for ever, Ailsa forced herself to sit up.

"I'm fine now. Thank you, Sir." She remembered to add the title. "I'll go and change."

Aidan stared at her. "Connie will go with you so you don't get lost."

And go where you shouldn't, was the inference. She'd sort out Connie when she had to. "Of course, Sir. Thank you."

Aidan lifted her off his lap and stood her onto the floor. "Why do I think you're up to something?" he asked rhetorically as Connie approached them. He patted Ailsa on her bum. "See you in the lounge area in a few minutes."

Ailsa nodded and followed Connie out of the dungeon. Once they were out of earshot of the men, Connie grabbed Ailsa by her blanket covered shoulder. "What are you going to say?"

"I've no idea." Ailsa opened the door to their changing room and began to throw her clothes on. Once she was covered, she leaned on the wall. "What are you?"

"Me? Oh fuck. You've dropped me in it as well, haven't you? Ross and I are just sorting things out, and now I've either got to lie to him and protect him, or compromise my job."

Ailsa looked at her white-faced companion. "Not necessarily. You can just say when you woke up I'd gone."

Connie blinked. "What do you mean by that, ma'am?"

So she was back to ma'am now. Ailsa decided that helped her to do what she was about to do.

"This." She clipped Connie on the jaw with her left fist and caught her as her head flipped backward and she lost consciousness. Yet again, Ailsa thanked the less than politically correct lessons she'd had the opportunity to attend and take heed of.

Ailsa slid the blanket she'd so recently had wrapped round herself under Connie's head, and looked around the room. In the corner was a neat pile of clean towels and she used a couple to tuck round Connie. She reckoned she had around five or six minutes to get away. Not long, but she could hide out in the passage or the lean-to if she had to. As long as she got into the passage without being found.

She left the room and made her way up the servants' stairs to the room where the entrance to the passage was situated. Luckily it was well away from the dungeon *and* she had remembered her way around the rebuilt castle from her previous investigations.

Within minutes, she slipped into the room she needed without meeting anyone. Somewhere nearby a phone rang. Ailsa worked the mechanism, slid through the gap in the wall even before the panel had stopped moving and pressed the knobs to close the aperture. There was a horrendous grinding noise and the panel stopped moving, leaving a three inch gap between the wall and the edge of the paneling.

Ailsa swore and tried to move it. No such luck. It seemed the aging mechanism had decided enough was enough. The only consolation was that if it was jammed where it was, no one would be able to follow her, unless they were a contortionist with an ability to get through such a tiny space. Nonetheless, she had no intention of chancing it. Fumbling slightly until she touched the webbing strap, Ailsa picked up her rucksack and felt her way to the top step. She daren't turn on her torch, just in case someone entered the room behind her. Instead of an empty room, it was furnished now and Ailsa had no idea who used it or when.

Resolutely she tried to ignore the thought of spiders, rats, bats and anything that might go bump in the night, and counted the steps as she moved downwards. By the time she got to the last one she was sweating, and she still had to venture out of the building and into the shed. Then the fun may well begin. The only plus point was that the lean-to was at the rear of the castle and it would take a while to reach it once Connie was discovered. Ailsa had to risk getting out and away.

She eased through the door in the castle wall, and shut it behind her. If they hadn't worked out where she'd disappeared to, she wasn't going to help them find out. It took a few moments to wriggle around the spades, hoes and other old gardening implements without disturbing them, before she was able to peer outside. As far as she could tell, the area was deserted.

Stay or go?

She went. With a speed born of desperation, Ailsa ran over the rough grass between the lean-to and the woods, and didn't stop to see if anyone had glimpsed her. She reached her car in a time an Olympic champion would be proud of, scrambled in and drove away as if the hounds of hell were after her.

Which in one way, she reckoned, they might well be.

Chapter Six

"So, they said everything was fine and let us home and aren't they cute?" Kath snuggled into the overlarge chair, and held a baby in each arm. She looked from one of her companions to another in turn. "I mean burps and poos aside, they are very well behaved. Of course they are *very* advanced for their age." She giggled. "How I hated our Aunt Gwenda who always said that about her children. Luckily she lived in Swansea and we lived up here so we didn't have to suffer her or her oh so advanced children very often. Tudor ended up in prison and Sioned ran away to be a hippy in Mallorca with a guy who already had five kids by four women. Mind you, I think Tudor is going straight now, which evidently is more than can be said of us. We have kinks. Okay," she said without taking a breath. "What aren't you telling me?"

Aidan, who was stroking the cheek of Lola — or was it Grey? Why couldn't Kath be stereotypical and dress one in pink and the other in blue, not both in red? — shrugged and looked toward Jeff. Jeff raised one eyebrow. Behind him, his twin Jess became busy pleating the curtains and David, her partner, leaned on the wall and crossed his arms.

"Look if something is going on that has you all talking in corners, and by all I include my so called best friend, and you're not telling me what it's all about then I will start to get mad," Kath said in such a sweet, saccharine voice Aidan had to stop his lips twitching. "And my milk might dry up, and Lola and Grey will suffer and you'll get no sleep, and I'll get crotchety and—"

"Okay, you blackmailer, you. You never know, you might have a theory all about it. Here, come to papa." Jeff took his son from his wife and began to stroll around the room. He handed him to Jess who went white before she took the baby and held him close. The look on her face defied description.

Grey gave a burp and farted.

The five adults in the room laughed and the tension eased. Even Jess relaxed and didn't hold Grey as if he were a time bomb.

"I guess it's partly down to me," Aidan said. "Well it could be, I honestly don't know. I'm thinking it's my bloody father again, but it's not quite his style. Too subtle for him. But when you went into labor something happened, which was nothing to do with any of you. Except for Jeff asking me to act for him."

"Clear as mud. Gah, you men are so pathetic at explaining anything except what you want your sub to do," Kath said in a voice Aidan knew was full of put-on pathos. "How about start at the beginning?"

That was the problem. "I would if I could, but to be honest, I'm not sure I really know where that is," Aidan said. "Apart from that, is it just one thing or lots? Well I'll give you my bit and we can try and sort out the jigsaw."

"Fair enough, but before we start, can someone bring me a laptop and a glass of water?" Kath asked. "And if you're going to cringe when I feed my children, now's the time to say so."

Behind her, Jess went pale, and David leaned forward to hug Jess and the baby. Jess leaned on him for a second.

"Here, take your godson for a while," Jess said and passed Grey to David. "He'll want his mummy in a sec, so there's no need to panic." Luckily the baby didn't seem to mind playing pass the parcel. "Jeff can get a laptop, he'll know which one better than any of us. I'll get water and coffee and stuff. Aidan, will you help me, please?"

"Sure." Aidan wondered why she'd asked him, but it was no big deal. He followed Jess out of the comfortable lounge of Kath and Jeff's apartment, and into their kitchen. He knew they were hoping to move into the house they were having built on the grounds of the castle before long, but a series of unusual occurrences and the indication that there had been intruders in the castle had delayed the move by several months. Neither Jeff nor Jess, who owned the castle between them, wanted to leave it empty overnight. However, as both owners were building new homes nearby, Aidan wondered what they would do once they were ready. Maybe employ a night watchman, or offer one or both of the flats to someone in the lifestyle.

"You're an artist, aren't you?" Jess asked as she piled soft drinks and water onto a tray along with dips, salad and crackers. "Could you sketch who you took to be Annabelle?"

"Annabelle?"

Jess leaned against the sink. "Oh, sorry, I forgot we hadn't got to that point yet. The sub from the night Kath went into labor. Her name is Annabelle. There was a message on the answering machine the next morning. She'd spent the evening in A & E at the local hospital with a friend who'd had a suspected heart attack. So the one thing we do know is your sub wasn't her. I wondered if you could sketch her, and we could see if we recognized who it was."

"Not a bad idea," Aidan said. "I'm no David Hockney, but I can get a rough idea. Do we have paper and charcoal?"

"Yep, I, shall we say, purloined some from uni a few weeks ago for something I was trying out for the students."

He remembered Jess was a lecturer there.

"It's still in my study. If you take this through, I'll grab it and bring it along. Oh and just so you don't accidentally put your foot in it, I love Jeff and Kath and my new niece and nephew to bits. But please don't ask David and me if we'll be next. I'm sterile." She turned and left the room in a hurry.

Deep in thought, Aidan picked up the tray. So that was why she'd looked as she had. Poor Jess, if indeed she did want children. Oh there were ways and means, but he could imagine that to see her best friend and brother with two healthy kids would bring out mixed feelings.

He walked back to the lounge, wondering about the low blows fate dealt people. He himself had never wanted to father a child. His own father's attitude had made sure of that. However, that was one thing. Finding out what Ailsa was up to was more important, and he'd do what he needed to do to help.

"Right, let's see." Aidan shut his eyes for a second to consider how he could portray Ailsa. "I'll only do a head sketch, but she wasn't very tall and had a nice shape. Not stick thin, not over heavy, just perfect." He colored and laughed self-consciously. "Busted. I must admit, I knew damn well she couldn't be your A, Jeff, because my first thought was that she was as green as grass. I bet everything she knew came from reading a novel. But she was an out and out sub, even if she didn't realize it. God, what I'd give for her to be on the level and want me as her Dom." He looked up from his sketching to see each of the others with a look of astonishment on their faces. "What's up?"

"Nothing, except you admitting you want someone as your sub," David answered him. "This from the man who is adamant he wants no ties."

"Yeah well, hasn't it hit all of us at one time? You think you're really happy, and then, wham, you find out you aren't. That something is missing and you don't realize it until it, or in my case she, appears and affects you like a punch in the gut."

"True," Kath said as she looked from one baby to another, where they slept side by side in two carrycots. "And I realize I need food. Or maybe gummy bears. Yep, definitely gummy bears, after all they're fruit flavored so they have to be one of my five a day, yes?"

"Sorry, honey. The clue is in the word flavor. Have some milk instead." Jeff handed her a glass.

Kath made realistic retching noises but drank the liquid and handed the glass back. Then she took up the laptop and began to type. "Okay, good to go. But I'd still like gummy bears."

Aidan laughed. "I'll buy you some in the village when I get my paper in the morning. How's that?"

"Good, thank you. Can you sketch and talk?"

"Of course. Right, so my father and his threats to us all." Rapidly Aidan spoke of his father's attitude and ultimatum. "I wondered at first if Ailsa had been sent by my father for some underhanded something. Then I accepted not even he could get things in place so fast."

"Ailsa?" Jess spoke for the first time since she'd returned to the lounge with the sketchpad and charcoal. She walked toward Aidan and peered over his shoulder.

He shaded part of the sketch, tore it off the pad and handed it to Jess. "She said her name was Alisa Mac something, and she used to know you. To be honest, there was so much going through my mind, I was more concerned with trying to fathom out why she was here, because I was damned sure it wasn't to sub, than listening to her name. I was somewhat annoyed and confused as well, because I thought Ross hadn't locked the door."

Jess picked up the sketch and took a brief look at it.

"Ailsa McLagan. I met her in the village a few weeks ago after not seeing her for years. We were friends when I lived here and… Fuck, shoot and bollocks. Oh, sorry, cover the babies' ears and don't wash my mouth out, Sir. She knows about the passage. We used to play in it as kids, and hide from Jeff in there because he could never find the mechanism. Is that it? Is it Ailsa who's been wandering around and checking out stuff? Why, though?"

Jeff took the sketch from her. "Are you sure this is your sometime mate? I don't recognize her."

"You wouldn't. You ignored her after she broke your spaceship, and Dad said you couldn't tie her up and spank her. Grief, I'd forgotten that. It seems you had Dominant tendencies even at nine."

Kath looked up from the laptop. "Before my time. We were in Stirling until I was about thirteen. There's no Ailsa McLagan on the members' list, I've checked. Nothing remotely like it."

"I didn't think there would be," Aidan said. "She was clueless. I pushed, went all out Dom and teased her as well, but if Ross and Connie hadn't come back then, I wouldn't have played. There's no way I'm causing any problems for Diomhair when some wannabe or not sub cries assault. Do you know anything about her now?"

Jess shook her head. "I hadn't even thought of her for years. When I saw her in the village I could have sworn she was as surprised as me to meet up. Is she on any social network, Kath?"

Kath pressed some keys on the laptop and shook her head. "Not that I can see. Mind you neither are you, and lots of teachers, police or firemen, et cetera, et cetera choose not to have a profile or go for something stupid. Hold on... Blimey, now then... Oh yes..." She typed rapidly. "Got you, you bitch. Well, I think so. Look." She turned the laptop toward the others.

As if on cue, one of the babies began to grizzle. "Grub time. I need to feed Lola, because as sure as eggs are eggs, Grey will wake up any –" A wail from the other baby made her pause. "Told you. Someone pass me Lola and cuddle Grey whilst I get Lola latched on, and then I can get him attached as well. What someone does with more than two children who want feeding, I have no idea."

Aidan went to the Moses baskets, and peered in. "Who is who? I'm a clueless male who needs visual confirmation as to who is a she and who is a he."

"The one red in the face and screaming like he hasn't been fed for a fortnight, which as he's only twelve days old is impossible, is of course Grey. Typical male. He'll have to wait. I got him latched on first last time."

It took a few seconds to sort out both babies. Then Kath looked up. "Well?"

"Like an old hand," Jess said. "Oh, you mean the article. Something's rotten in the state of Denmark. Well, in the district of here anyway."

David whistled. "A policewoman, eh? Decorated for bravery and an inspector to boot. Now why didn't we know that?"

"Because she isn't a member," Aidan said. "Where's the entrance to the passage?"

"Leading question—and I feel sorry for your sub if you don't know that," Jeff replied and burst out laughing. "Sorry, couldn't resist. It's in the room we store furniture and use as an extra lounge if we need it. In what was David's flat before we configured stuff. But damned if I can work the mechanism. Even now."

"You lot go and play detective," Kath said. "Then come back and tell me what you find. I'll get these two settled then we can have food and plot."

Chapter Seven

"Aidan, there's a policeman here who wants to talk to you." Jackie poked her head around his office door. "You forgotten to pay a parking fine?"

Aidan shook his head, although the way his mind had been working lately, he reckoned it could have happened. He checked the time. Almost five. Where had the day, or even the last week or so, gone? He needed to get his act together, forget about missing subs, and move on. It wasn't easy, though, not when a certain scent, or a woman with short blonde hair, made his heartbeat speed up and his Dom side itch to punish someone. No, not someone, just her.

"Aidan?"

He'd forgotten Jackie was waiting for a reply. "Sorry, Jacks, I was wool gathering. Not that I know of. What's his name?"

Jackie snorted. "Chauvinist. He's a she, an Inspector McLagan."

"Well, well." Aidan pushed his chair back from the desk and tucked his T-shirt into his jeans. The anger that filled him surprised him, especially as he was wise enough to accept that it stemmed from hurt. "Tell her I'm busy."

"It's an inspector of the police, Aidan." *And needs to be seen*, her tone implied.

"So? I guess she pees, farts and tells lies like the rest of us. I'm busy. End of." Aidan stood up and waved his hands in the general direction of the outer office, even though the door between it and him was closed. "It's almost time to shut up shop for the week. I have work to do so I can go home with a clear conscience. I'm serious, Jacks. I have no time for her." *Not now, not ever.* "Any explanations or questions can be made in writing to Diomhair, not me."

Jackie's eyes widened, but she merely nodded and shut the door behind her. She knew enough about Aidan's life to know what Diomhair was.

Within a few seconds, the door opened. As Aidan expected, his visitor was known to him.

"Well, what have we here?" He knew his tone bordered on insolent and his visitor reddened. "It's the wannabe, lying through her teeth, not really a sub, who doesn't listen when she's told I'm busy, big lady policewoman. So, Inspector, what can I do for you?"

Her face was the color of the knickers he'd caught a glimpse of all those weeks ago.

"Cut the crap, be an adult and let me explain, maybe? Or is your dick in an 'I am the boss' mode and not going to give in?" Her tone was scathing.

Well that was coming to the point with a vengeance. Aidan felt about two inches tall and ashamed, but not for long. She was the one in the wrong, not him.

"Fuck you."

Much to his surprise she giggled, and looked a lot less austere, and more like the lady he'd topped.

"I so hope so."

"Well, maybe." His respect for her, although grudging, crept up a few notches. "Now it's 'put your cards on the table' time. Who the hell are you?" God, how it hurt to ask that. Aidan would have loved to continue whatever charade she had played, and see just how far she was prepared to continue, but not when the reputation of Diomhair was at stake. "You lied."

She dipped her head in agreement. "I did. But in my defense, I was at work. Legal and signed off by the necessary people to allow me to in effect break in. Yes, it can be done legally. It doesn't happen often, and it has to be agreed by the Advocate General, but in certain circumstances, it's agreed on. This was one of those times."

Aidan shut his mouth and bit back the sneering retort he had been about to make.

"Like it or not, you, all of you, were suspects. Now you're not. Not even your father, although I would like a few words with him over some asshat who works for him and alleged intimidation. But that can wait. However, I have permission to talk. It'll be up to you where we go, if anywhere. But can you get me a chance to speak to the owners and so on?"

"Are you going to let me be a Dom? Play and screw?" He cringed at his crudity. To his astonishment she laughed.

"Maybe. Who knows? If you give me a good reason."

Aidan gave in to temptation. Sod it. He'd pay the price later—if he had to. Maybe she had her handcuffs with her...

He grabbed Ailsa by the shoulders, kissed her hard on the mouth and drew back before she had time to respond. Her eyes were bright, and even from such a short contact, her skin was flushed. As she didn't kick him in the balls or punch him in the face, Aidan took it as a good sign, spun her round and began to bend her over his desk.

"Aidan, is everything okay?" Jackie's voice came over the intercom.

Shit. He'd been so caught up in the moment he'd forgotten Jackie was next door, and liable to enter at any minute.

Ailsa giggled. He put his hand over her mouth and almost groaned when she sucked, licked and nipped the soft flesh of his palm.

"Yeah, the inspector and I are old friends, with business to sort out. We'll be a while, so er, you can knock off now. Just lock the door behind you."

Jackie sniggered. "That's one way of putting it I guess. Okay, enjoy sorting, and see you on Monday." She clicked the intercom off and a few seconds later he heard the main door bang. Evidently Jackie had been ready to leave on time.

"Now where were we?"

"Mrmp nmdrd," Ailsa said behind his hand.

"Really? Is that cop speak for a punishment spanking? I reckon I can obli— Fuck it, Ailsa, that hurt." She'd bitten his palm, hard. He removed it from her mouth, and inspected the puncture holes. "If you were my sub, you'd not sit down for a week after that. You really do need to learn how to give respect."

"Ha. Pot, kettle and black." Ailsa twisted around and leaned back on the desk. "You have to give it to get it."

She had a point.

Aidan picked up one of her curls and wound it around his finger. "True enough. So shall we start the last ten minutes again? I was an arse, granted, but I never, ever lied about who I was."

"And I did, yes." She leaned into his hand. "I'm more sorry than you'll ever know, I had to do that. However, like I told you, I was at work and there were extenuating circumstances. So do you give me the chance to explain to everyone involved?" She straightened up, but not enough to dislodge his hand.

"Do you give me the chance to take you? However I want? Now?"

Why was he pushing her like that? *Because I want her submission. All of it.*

"Is this 'you show me yours and I'll show you mine' time?" Ailsa's voice was laced with humor. "I've read up on safe words and stuff. I'm not as green as I was. Or maybe that should be I'm more green? Anyway, what do you want?" She paused and very slowly dipped her head, then looked up to stare him directly in the eyes before she briefly closed one eyelid. "Sir."

Aidan grinned. This could be fun. His body was taut with the thrum of anticipation that rushed through him and his dick swelled and hardened under its cover of denim.

"What I want to do is bend you over the desk and rip off anything that hides you from me. Lift your skirts, tie your hands and feet so you're nicely spread-eagled and open for me, and spank your arse until it's rosy red and warm. But I won't, not yet, not until you're willing to see if we have the makings of a good Dom/sub relationship, and I know what was going on. What I will do is ask you if I can make love to you. Here, now and, yeah, probably over the desk."

Where had the words come from? Aidan was damned sure he hadn't been going to say that. However, he admitted that he wanted her in any way possible, and he wasn't going to even try the Dom/sub route until everything had been explained. Why he thought making love was different he didn't know. It didn't mean any less than dominating her, it was just different.

Her eyes widened and again her skin suffused with color. She opened her mouth, closed it and swallowed.

"How?"

"Oh, the usual way, cock in pussy, with a condom. Nothing weird or untoward." Aidan cringed once more at the words he'd spoken. He was usually a little less crude. "Sorry," he apologized. "That's crass. I'm off-kilter more than I thought, it seems. But I do want to make love with you and I do have protection." He blessed the action that had him picking up a pack of condoms along with his meal deal at lunchtime. "I want to get to know you."

Ailsa was silent for the best part of a minute. She nibbled her thumb, and he bit back the words to tell her to stop. Then, slowly, she pushed herself upright and smiled.

"Well now, Sir. Personally I don't think we can have one thing without the other. I researched you. It's amazing what you can find out when you have the might of a national government department's computer behind you. And it all came up good. The one thing I did find, from various 'I never divulge my sources' places, was that you are a Master. More than a Dom, a good person to teach me all I want to know, and you don't have a sub. Well, I'd like to make that maybe you don't." She slid to her knees and bent her head as she put her hands behind her. "I'm off duty now, Sir, and would ask if you'll help me. Please show me how to be a good sub."

Aidan looked down at the top of her head. Her golden curls shined in the evening sunlight that streamed through the window with tiny motes of dust in its rays.

"Any sub? Or my sub? What if I say I don't want a sub?" He tugged her hair until she looked up.

"Then I'll say no thank you, Sir. Leave now and next time you see me it will be in an official capacity as I speak to those involved with Diomhair. I might be clueless, which you know anyway, but I am interested. However, it seems I'm like a baby duckling. Fixated on the first thing, or person, I saw that interested me in the lifestyle."

Aidan laughed. "I've never been a duckling's Sir before. I guess that makes our safe word quack then." He sobered. "Are you sure? I don't want a twenty-four seven lifestyle, and I don't think you do. But I do want to be sure that if we learn we're right for each other, we both want the same thing. So let's start by me saying, now, pet. Can you ride pillion?"

Ailsa looked down at her pencil skirt and killer heels. Aidan reckoned she'd worn them as a confidence booster. For him, it made him ache to see what she wore underneath.

"I'd rather drive, than be driven in this case. But yes, I can ride pillion, even dressed like this."

"Good, then let's go. I think we'd be better off somewhere more comfortable. Where's your car?"

"At home. I got a lift and said I'd ring if I needed a ride anywhere later. But as of twenty minutes ago, I'm a free woman until eight a.m. on Monday, so" — she spread her hands wide — "I'm all yours."

"Trusting."

Ailsa shook her head. "Not really. Three people know where I am. One can track me, and I probably know as much about you as you do yourself."

"Then take your underwear off and get ready to ride pillion."

She shook her head and slowly lifted the edge of her skirt above her thighs so the lacy tops of her stockings showed.

"I can't do that."

Aidan's heart plummeted and a heavy lump of disappointment wedged deep in his stomach. So much for saying she wanted to sub. Was it all just a game to her?

"Why not? It's not much to ask, and as my sub you'll not wear underwear unless I say so."

"That's a relief, Sir. However, I can't take my underwear off for a very good reason." She opened the top three buttons of her fine silk blouse, and let the sides gape until the valley between her breasts showed. Naked and braless. Then very deliberately, she turned her back on him and lifted the hem of her skirt higher until the tops of her legs were exposed and the edge of her rear showed.

"You see, Sir, with regards to underwear? I'm not wearing any."

Chapter Eight

The way Aidan's eyes widened and he blinked, just once, gave Ailsa hope. Hope that he'd understand and let her play.

It had been a long week or so, talking and arguing with her boss, and finding out that whatever they were looking for had nothing to do with the owners or, as far as they could tell, the users of Diomhair. Not to mention discovering that Aidan's father was only just on the right side of shady in his business practices. No wonder Aidan had been so wary. Oh, his father hadn't broken any laws, but he wasn't always totally open and honest about any pitfalls that might occur. Then a chat with someone called Lynette had given her another reason for Aidan's unease. Finally, she'd gotten the agreement that she should be the one to explain and see if Jeff and co could help.

Ailsa had been adamant it was Aidan to whom she would speak first, and Cameron had agreed with a cryptic, "He's the one for you."

Now she waited impatiently to see what Aidan would say or do. Ailsa knew one thing about herself.

As much as she thought submitting to Aidan was right for her, her besetting sin was impatience. Even when she'd wriggled out of her bra and pants in the ladies' loo at work, and stuffed them into her bag, she'd rushed to get the job done. Mind you, she thought now, half of that was worry in case her braless boobs swung around under the severe cut of her pinstriped work jacket. Then she'd tapped her fingers impatiently on the dashboard as the young PC had driven her out of the city. Poor boy, he was new and nervous about driving her, especially, as he put it, into the wilds. That worried her somewhat, as the village she was heading to wasn't much more than half an hour from the city. How would he cope if he really had to drive into the countryside and navigate the single track roads? It was a wonder he'd been passed to drive anything other than a pushbike.

He'd hesitated at a junction, even though there was nothing in view for several hundred yards. Ailsa had bitten back a sigh. She was not good at waiting for anything. Even though she was afraid that once she reached her destination she might not get a happy outcome, now she'd gotten permission to tell everything she wanted to get it over and done with.

Could her attitude be reconciled with submitting? Maybe only Aidan could answer that.

Now, waiting for Aidan's answer, Ailsa counted to ten under her breath. Then to ten again. Damn him. If he wanted her to say or do something so he could play the punishment card she'd be quacking 'red' like every duck in the pond was in full voice.

"I like that," he said just as she was ready to scream and shout at the top of her voice. He picked up a leather jacket, soft with age, from the back of his chair, and slung it over one arm. "Let's go."

His hand was warm on her back as he urged her toward the door. Ailsa thought it was almost a brand. That when she took her clothes off, the imprint of his hand would be seared onto her lower back. Strangely it didn't faze her.

The familiar scent of leather and the hint of a citrus cologne teased her nostrils. Suddenly she realized why it *was* so familiar. She'd scented it at Diomhair the night he'd shown her what could be in their future – if they had one.

It took every ounce of her determination not to ask where they were going. If her boss trusted him, why shouldn't she? Deep down Ailsa knew, whether Cameron did or not, something about this man screamed integrity and honesty to her. Even if after she'd done more research she'd accepted he'd been pushing and teasing her at Diomhair before Connie and the other guy – Ross, she remembered – had returned.

The big, powerful motorbike parked in a courtyard at the rear of the building took her breath away. Talk about something throbbing between your legs. Every hot erotic book she'd read flashed through her mind. One in particular, where someone had ridden a motorbike knickerless and had an orgasm. Was it possible? Maybe she'd get to find out.

Aidan shrugged his jacket on before he unlocked a box on the back and took out two helmets.

"Here you go." He fitted it over Ailsa's head and adjusted it, before putting on one similar. "Hop on." The gleam in his eyes told her Aidan understood she was going to show a lot more of herself than was polite in public.

She'd show him all right. Once committed, Ailsa gave her all. Well she admitted she hoped she did –

she was still a bit hazy on what she was committing to and what the all was. Ailsa put her bag over her shoulder and with what she hoped was a sultry smile—although what a sultry smile was, was anyone's idea—she hitched her skirt as high as she could without baring rather too much of her body.

She eyed the bike doubtfully. What if she kicked it and it fell over? Could she really lift her leg high enough to get it over the seat? An old cricket report where someone had tried to jump the wickets and the commentator said 'he can't get his leg over' came to mind and she giggled.

"Okay, I'll fall for it. What's funny?" Aidan asked as he stood next to her and waited for her to do as he asked.

"Can I get my leg over?"

He laughed. "Any time, pet. Lift the skirt higher. There's only me here to see, and I'll get on the bike first to spare your blushes." The words 'this time' were unsaid but definitely there. He did as he said, and his long, leather clad back was presented to her.

But he'll still maybe get an eyeful when I get off. Am I ready for that? Whether she was or not, Ailsa accepted it was going to happen. She took a deep breath, looked away from Aidan and hitched the hem even further until it was bunched around her waist.

"If I ladder these stockings, you owe me a new pair," she said in a warning voice as she twisted to stand sideways on to the bike, measured the height and did a high kick any chorus girl would be proud of. The breeze teased her bared-to-the-world pussy. Once her leg was well clear of the bike, she slid onto the saddle.

The leather was cold on her bum, and the slight rise between her and the front half of the seat rubbed closely over her clit. Ailsa was uncomfortably aware of just how sensitive she felt. She did her best to pull her skirt lower but without much luck, so twisted her bag forward instead and rested it over her pussy.

Aidan laughed. "Spoilsport." His voice reverberated around inside the helmet, and Ailsa realized they were wired to hear and speak to each other.

"You looked," she said and poked him in the back. "In your mirrors."

"Of course I did. And from now on, pet, this is our scene. Next poke gets you more than a poke back. Understand?" He didn't wait for her answer and started the engine. "Hold on."

The bike moved forward and as it gathered speed, Ailsa held onto Aidan around his waist. The action dragged her uncovered body closer to his leather and denim covered one, the material rubbed over her, to sting and create an arousing friction. Ailsa tightened her grip. If she fell off it wouldn't be just her knees she skinned.

They left the courtyard and drove down the village high street. Ahead of them, Ailsa saw a police car outside the village policeman's house. She shut her eyes, because she didn't even want to know if it was occupied. Hopefully the helmet would hide just who was riding pillion bare-arsed.

As they left the village and the wind chilled her skin, Ailsa hoped it wouldn't be too long until they reached their destination. A blue body and chattering teeth wasn't the look she wanted to portray.

The bike gripped the road as Aidan expertly guided it around the bends and twists between his office and wherever they were going. Ailsa knew the roads and guessed which village they were heading toward, but from there? She had no idea and she'd valiantly not looked his address up. Now she wished she hadn't been quite so honorable.

"Five minutes. You okay?" His voice startled her. Ailsa had forgotten the mic in her helmet.

"Yes, fine if a bit draughty."

He chuckled. "I'll soon have you warmed up." His tone sounded as if it wasn't going to be merely via a hug. Ailsa began to tingle, and she tightened her inner muscles. Getting excited on the back of a motorbike might be one way of climaxing, but she didn't think she was ready for that, however much she'd liked reading about it. One thing at a time.

Aidan slowed the bike and turned up a driveway bordered by rhododendron bushes. "Bit bumpy here, too much rain and it's washed the gravel into humps and lumps that I've not had time to smooth out. Hold on tight." The bike lurched from one dip to the next and waves of dirty water washed out of the puddles. Ailsa was glad she wasn't walking through them.

"What the...?" Aidan swore, as he stopped the bike next to a large four-by-four. Ailsa watched with interest as a swarthy overweight man got out of one side, and a slimmer clone from the other.

"My father and goodness knows who. It's gonna be nasty." Aidan got off the bike and stood between Ailsa and the men. "Can you get off and, er, adjust your skirt? Christ I'm so sorry. If I'd have known the arsehole was going to appear, I'd not have brought you."

"Don't worry." Ailsa slid off the bike and pulled her skirt down in one swift movement. "And I'm glad he's here. I'm going to put the fear of God in him." She waited until Aidan lifted both their helmets off and ran her fingers through her hair. Luckily, as it was short and curly, she knew from experience it wouldn't look too messy.

"Do you want me to see what's going on, Sir?" She used the title deliberately, and some of the bleakness that had shown in Aidan's eyes disappeared. "Or shall we give him enough rope to hang himself?"

Aidan smiled. "Oh, definitely the latter. Can we?"

"Oh, I think so. I'll let you start, Sir."

He winked. "Thank you for that, pet. Let's get shot of him as soon as possible. I have a bed, a blindfold, some beautifully soft handcuffs and a nice teasing flogger with your name on waiting inside."

For once the thought of being unsighted and bound didn't worry her. Instead it set off ripples of arousal and tingles deep inside. Ailsa tamped down the sensations and watched as Aidan approached his father.

"Father."

"This is Sergeant Franklin." The older man didn't bother with platitudes or greetings. "He wants to ask a few questions about your lifestyle. If you promise to give it up and sign this" — Murison Jefferies waved a paper in front of him — "he'll keep you out of it. You can have your old job back then."

Ailsa kept her face straight with difficulty. Really the man had been watching too many old '70s cop show reruns. It was obvious Aidan thought so too, because he laughed.

"Pull the other one. He's about as much a policeman as I am." He turned to the slimmer man. "Show me your warrant card."

The man jutted his chin out. "You don't make the demands, mate."

Ailsa decided it was time to intervene. She took three steps forward, and saw Aidan grin. "Over to you, pet," he said under his breath. "He's no policeman, is he?"

Ailsa shook his head. If he were, then she'd turn her warrant card in as soon as she could. He was the type who'd give the force a bad name.

"Maybe he doesn't make the demands, *mate,* but I do." She stood square on to the man. "Show me your warrant card."

"Ha, some alleged Dom you are. Hiding behind a woman. Or is she the Domme, eh?" Murison Jefferies sneered the words. "Some women want a prick."

"Well they'd get one if they were with you, wouldn't they? And not in the 'nice big cock and know what to do with it' way." Ailsa wondered where that crudity had come from. However, she didn't give him a chance to interrupt. "Mind you, I suppose in one way I *am* in charge. I'm the policewoman." Ailsa took her warrant card from her bag. "Inspector McLagan. I'm so pleased to meet you, Mr Jefferies. Some of my colleagues want a chat with you. And if this is Ronald Franklin, they'd like to chat to him as well."

Chapter Nine

If looks could kill, Aidan reckoned he'd be ten feet under and someone would be praying for his soul. He'd bet his new violet wand it wouldn't be his father. That man stared at them both and turned back to his car.

"Bollocks. I'm a legitimate businessman, and that's all there is to it."

"Of course you are," Ailsa said cheerfully. "But is he?" She waved one hand at Franklin who glared, got into the vehicle beside him and folded his arms. Murison Jefferies didn't reply to her. He turned to Aidan, his face red, and the veins on his forehead bulged.

Aidan wondered if there really was such a thing as dying by apoplexy.

"You're screwed, just like your mother." Murison Jefferies swung himself into the driver's seat of the four-by-four, which swayed on its springs. Then he drove off, scattering gravel everywhere. Aidan resigned himself to a blunt lawnmower.

"Didn't you want to question them or something?" Aidan asked as the car turned out of the drive. "Stick bamboo under their fingernails and use a violet wand somewhere it would hurt? I've got a new one, as of yet unused."

"Nope, it was all bluff. Why waste a violet wand on those two? If they're all I've read they are, it's much too good to use like that. Sadly they did nothing wrong. If you notice, he didn't say a sergeant of what, and nor did Franklin. And Franklin was a sergeant in the army years ago. Plus, all Franklin is wanted for is a parking offense. Your father is an unpleasant individual, with some serious issues about BDSM, but that's not a crime. He's just not someone I'd ever choose to spend time with. And I'd count my fingers after shaking hands with him. I reckon he's very much in favor of something for nothing."

"Yeah, you've sussed him out." Aidan ran his hand over her cheek. "I've no idea what that cryptic comment about Mum was, but I must ask her if she knows just what he's harping on about. As far as I know, she just left him when I did, and she's now loving life in Lanzarote. Not now, though. Later." He took Ailsa's chin between his thumb and forefinger and used the same finger to lift her jaw upwards, until her head was tilted back. She smiled and lowered her eyelids, which wouldn't be easy at the angle he had her head tilted to.

"So, pet. Are you ready to play? If we do decide we want to go further, usually play won't start until we're in the playroom. But today, I really want to start now. Shall we?"

Aidan took a deep breath and filled his lungs with fresh—tinged sadly with the aroma of muck-spreading—country air and waited with as much patience as he could dredge up for Ailsa to reply. The breeze touched her curls and they stretched out from her skull in a yellow, dancing halo.

"Yes, Sir."

Her eyes glittered and her breathing was shallow and rapid. So she was interested, really interested and it hadn't all been a lie. That thought gave him a warm, satisfied feeling. As did the fact that she trusted him enough to play there and then.

"Then play now, talk later." He took hold of her by the hand and led her toward the door. "Once I open this, I want you to go upstairs and into the first room on the left. It has a bathroom, so use what you need, strip and greet me on your knees sat beside the bed, facing the door. You have around five minutes." He had a thought. "Are your knees healed?"

"Oh yes, Sir." She walked past him and very slowly with a deliberate wriggle began to climb the stairs. Aidan wolf-whistled and Ailsa looked over her shoulder at him.

"Thank you, Sir. I aim to please." She ran her finger down between the sides of her shirt, and opened the few jacket buttons that were still fastened.

"Minx." He watched as she took the last few stairs in the same deliberate manner, and turned through the doorway he'd indicated, before he took out his phone.

A piece of material floated down the stairwell. Aidan picked up the silky blouse and twirled it on his finger. He was going to enjoy himself. It seemed Ailsa had hidden depths she'd not allowed to show before. Well, he reasoned, it would have been difficult when she was at work and he was pushing her as hard as he could. This time he intended for them both to savor the give and take.

Almost five minutes to the second later he switched his phone to silent, and turned off the ringer on the landline. His playroom was reasonably soundproof, but he didn't want any distractions for either of them.

As he approached the bedroom door, he wondered what he'd find. He'd made the deliberate decision to ask Ailsa to go in there and not the other room. He wanted to be with her when she saw the playroom for the first time. As playrooms went, it was mild, not much more than a spare room with a few extras, but even so in no way could it be called vanilla.

Aidan turned the handle and opened the door. The sight of Ailsa waiting for him as he'd directed stole his breath away.

In the mirror behind her he could see her skin was tanned with two pale strips across her back and her ass. The contrast made him itch to redden the paleness of her rear, and scribe his thoughts over her back. Perhaps one day he'd have the chance.

"That's perfect, pet. What color are you?"

"Green, Sir."

His cock hardened at those two words, and silently he unsnapped the top of his jeans and removed his shirt.

"And how do you feel about a little flogging? Just a gentle kiss of the leather on you." He opened a cupboard by the door to the bathroom and took out a soft leather flogger that he knew would kiss the skin, sting for a second and leave any sub wondering what next. It made a nice swish as he tested the throw.

"Yellow, Sir, but only because it's all so new." She didn't lift her head and mumbled in the direction of his feet.

Aidan hunkered down and tugged her hair. "Look at me, pet. You trust me, or you wouldn't be here." He didn't make it a question. "You can cry red, or quack if you prefer" — he chuckled and she gave a little giggle — "at any time. It's only going to be twenty, hardly enough to get the glow. I'd like to take you into the playroom, but I'm not going to."

She looked up at him so fast it was a wonder he didn't hear bones crack.

"Why not, um, Sir?"

"Because I want to redden your arse and then make love to you. If we go next door I'll want to scribe you, and I don't think you're ready for that."

She paled and swallowed.

"No, I thought not. Therefore, bend over the bench over there and put your hands into the shackles. Feet likewise."

Ailsa complied with alacrity, and Aidan went into full-on Dom mode. This was his life, his choice and him.

Within seconds he had her fastened, and took out a long strip of silk from his pocket. Without a word, he wrapped it across her eyes several times and fastened it behind her head.

"Color?"

"Green." She sounded surprised that he'd asked.

"Green what, pet?"

He wondered if she'd reply as grass, or grow the rushes oh, but she snapped back at him.

"Oh, hell, sorry, Sir. Green, Sir. I'm crap at this. You might as well just give up."

Aidan spoke softly into her ear. "That won't work, pet. You want to sub, or you wouldn't be here like this. It's a learning curve, and I won't start punishment for things like forgetting the Sir, yet." He blew into her ear and she squirmed. "Not until tomorrow." He stood up and let the strands of the flogger trail over her back and across her rear. "Now, count." He brought the strips of leather down onto her arse, hard enough to make her gasp, not too hard to put her off. The second stroke he knew would sting a little more. She still didn't speak so he added a third on top of the first. Already a nice gentle glow was appearing on her skin. He loved seeing it, and knew damn well his dick—which he often thought had a mind of its own—would be trying to peer over the top of his jeans, and adding pre-cum to his sweat slicked skin.

"Count or I'll have to start again."

"Eh?" Her voice was slurred.

"Count the strokes, pet. Let the sting play with you, but count the strokes." He swung the flogger. "Like this, one."

"One," she repeated the word.

With each stroke he chose the landing spot with care and consideration, and increased the pressure. After each set of two, he rubbed her arse, which he reckoned would be getting tender. By twenty he knew the sting would be harder, prolonged and leave more of a mark. He'd deliberately underplayed the results when he'd reassured her earlier. There was no need to enable panic to set in.

Ailsa counted out the hits in a steady voice, and when they got to twenty, Aidan put the flogger down, untied her and held her close. She gave a shudder, as he wrapped her in a soft mohair throw he'd left handy.

"Well done, pet. I'm proud of you."

"Really? I didn't do much." She snuggled into him and rested her head on his sweaty chest.

"You did, you know." Aidan handed her a sports bottle of water, and wiped the bits of chest he could reach with a towel. "Here, sips, not gulps, please. You took those blows like a pro. I'm going to enjoy seeing how far I can push you."

Ailsa sipped some water and held the bottle out to him. "Thank you. You know it's such a relief just to let you take control. I have to make decisions all day at work, some which aren't very nice. To know you've taken our decisions out of my hands, that my only job is to obey you, well it's a real turn-on. The minute you say pet to me, I go all gooey inside, and want to roll over for my tummy to be tickled." She giggled. "Or it seems my arse to be spanked. Me who hates nicknames like pet, or lamb and stuff. Now I don't even mind being bound, and ever since my cousin Sandra tied me to a tree and left me when we were playing cowboys and Indians the thought has terrified me. I was there for what seemed like hours. Mum said it was twenty minutes, because Sandra had forgotten where I was."

Aidan laughed. "I'd never forget you."

"Mmm, I know, Sir. I trust you."

"If I say, pet, now I'm going to make love to you?"

"Definitely then, Sir. Yes, please, Sir. As long…" she hesitated.

He knew what she was going to say. "With protection. Every time."

She let her breath out in a long whoosh. "Thank you. What would you like me to do?"

Aidan stood up and put her down carefully onto the mattress. She gasped when her bum met the cold covers and winced. "Ouch. Blimey that nips."

"Roll onto your tummy, and when you're ready, get onto your knees. I'm going to get some cream to rub in and then I'm going to take you from behind. Oh, don't worry."

She'd got halfway into the position he'd demanded, stiffened and turned to look at him. He understood the questioning look on her face.

"No anal, pet. Not yet. I think a sore arse on the outside is enough for you to cope with for now. Yes?"

"Yes, Sir." The relief was evident. *It seems anal needs to be discussed.* Aidan filed that information away, to be discussed at a later date. If Ailsa didn't like it, he'd do his damnedest to change her mind. It struck him how little they knew about each other, but how accepting they'd become in such a short time. Was that a good thing? Only time would tell.

He patted her bottom gently. "Breathe and relax, lie down if you want. I won't be a second."

He went into his playroom via the narrow door at the side of his bed, tugged off his jeans and picked up the lotion he wanted, along with some condoms. His cock was hard and jutted out from its bed of hair, swaying as he walked. Aidan gathered the droplets of pre-cum on the head and licked them absently. Next time he hoped it would be Ailsa that gathered them and tasted them, not him.

When he returned to the bedroom, she was flat on her tummy. As he approached the bed, she went onto her knees and rested her head on a pillow.

Aidan smoothed the cooling lotion over her reddened arse.

"Hmm, that feels so good, Sir." Her voice was soft and sleepy.

He ran his fingers between her legs and rubbed her clit. She was wet, and when he put one finger inside her, she clenched her muscles to hold him there. Aidan pulled the digit out and she moaned. He pinched her clit, just enough for her to hiss.

He chuckled. "I've got something better, pet." Aidan made short shrift of donning a condom. Next time he'd ask her to do the honors—however, this time he knew fine well he'd not last if she touched his cock.

"Open your legs a bit, yes like that, good girl."

She moved her knees apart. With infinite care, Aidan guided his cock into her then waited for Ailsa to adjust to the intrusion.

She sighed and she sounded so satisfied that Aidan rested on one hand and used the other to pinch the nearest nipple.

"Don't fall asleep," he teased her, and she snorted.

"Not much likelihood of… Ohh my, no definitely no likelihood."

Aidan began to move inside her. With each thrust she pushed back into him, clenching her muscles to increase the friction. He blessed the time he'd used to strengthen his arm muscles and still only using one hand for balance began to play with her clit, alternating between rubbing and nipping the sensitive nub.

"Ohh, aahh, sheesh, I'm going to come." Ailsa's agonized moan was enough for Aidan to know they'd be neck and neck in the coming stakes. Now wasn't the time to practice orgasm denial.

"Come then."

Oh how he wanted to hold back. To build the tension and add to the heat and pain and tingles and sheer exuberance that hit him, and share every last experience with Ailsa. But that was as useless as an ice cube in a hotpot. He couldn't help himself. Her touch, and her presence, took precedence over everything else. He had to move in her, to accept the way her muscles held him and relaxed to let him glide slowly then faster as he filled her channel. Light flashed in front of his eyes, and their scents and musky arousal filled his nostrils, edging him ever nearer the abyss.

Aidan bowed to the inevitable and gave one last powerful thrust into her. His orgasm ripped through him like an express train through a tunnel.

"Nooo... Yess... Shit, ohh grief, yeesss..." Ailsa stiffened and cried out, before she began to shake and slip forward onto the mattress.

For a brief moment, Aidan gave himself the luxury of slumping on top of her, before he lifted himself slightly.

Ailsa moaned her annoyance. "I like you there."

"I'll squash you, pet. And anyway, we have places to go and people to see. This was a quickie I couldn't resist." He pulled out of Ailsa and rolled off the bed. "I'll go and dispose of the condom, and then the bathroom is all yours."

"Can't we share?" she called after him. "The bathroom, not the condom, you can get rid of that now."

Aidan grinned as he flushed the condom away, had the shortest shower on record then stuck his head through the doorway. Ailsa was still slumped on her tummy, although her head was turned toward him.

"It's an economy," she said. "I bet you're on a water meter."

He shook his head. "Nice try, but not this time. We have to be at Diomhair in thirty minutes. They're waiting for us."

"What? And you let me rest when I could have been doing something?" She scrambled up off the bed, no trace of the sleepy sub left. "Are there towels and stuff out? And a shower cap?"

"Yes and yes, and it's only a ten minute ride, we've ages."

Ailsa turned and glared at him.

"Not when you don't want to look thoroughly Dommed and sexually sated." She disappeared into the bathroom, banged the door shut and the sound of the shower on full filtered through the wood.

Aidan grinned as he donned a clean T-shirt and jeans, and raised his voice. "Why not? They all know what it looks like."

The water went off and Ailsa appeared swathed in a towel.

"Exactly. I need to be professional. It's hard when everyone else in the room is imagining me as a tied down sub with a red arse and stripes on my back, or more."

She had a point. Aidan went to make some coffee and ring his mum.

Chapter Ten

Ailsa reckoned it was in deference to the fact that she needed to look tidy and professional that instead of guiding her toward the bike, Aidan handed her an insulated mug of coffee and an oat bar — "To keep your strength up until we get fed" — and took her to the garage, where a top of the range sports car sat. With the top up.

With a wink and a bow, Aidan opened the door and helped her into the low-slung passenger seat.

She stroked the soft leather interior. "Oh nice, I love leather." The car had the scent of new hide and wood found in vehicles that weren't used a lot. Ailsa inhaled deeply and sighed. "Oh, yes."

"Good, because I have a fancy to see you in a leather bustier and thong someday. Have you fastened your seatbelt?" Aidan glanced down at her, and seeing she had, set the car in motion.

Ailsa was sure her mouth was wide open like a fish at his words. Bustier in leather? Oh my.

"What did you say to Jeff and the others?" She couldn't say anything about leather bustiers. Even rolling the words around in her mind was orgasm-inducing. "Who is going to be there?"

"Jeff and Kath, Jess and David. They're the people who own and run Diomhair. No one else needs to be involved in anything else yet."

That was a relief. Ailsa didn't really want to have to involve Connie if she didn't have to.

She looked out of the window with interest. The distance to Diomhair wasn't far, but she guessed in the sports car, Aidan would have to be careful which roads he chose. A lot of the smaller ones would cause the car to bottom out on the bumps and holes. Each time she'd been to Diomhair it had been by a circuitous route. It was a novelty to turn up the main drive and enter the estate that way.

"Who lives there?" she asked as they passed a tiny cottage with an overgrown garden.

Aidan took a brief glance toward the stone building. "No one as yet. It's been empty for ages, ever since the old couple that used to 'do' for Jeff and Jess' parents moved into Aberfoyle and as they put it 'a wee bitty civilization'. As Mairi says, now she has the library van, the doctors and the store all within walking distance. They offered it to me, but I'm settled where I am. Why?"

"There was a white van parked behind it last time I was here. But I thought the place seemed deserted."

"It is, and we'll need to look into it. We've had problems. I honestly thought it was all down to you. Now I know it wasn't. Well, I reckon it isn't. Oh and guess what? I rang mum. We didn't have long to chat, but she's been keeping a secret for years." He paused and began to whistle.

"And? Or is not for my ears?"

Aidan laughed. "Oh it is. It seems Dad is so anti-kink and all things BDSM because mum is a Domme. As she put it, 'Your dad's got about as much authority in the bedroom as a drunken gnat, and resents it'. He hated her taking charge, but wouldn't or couldn't do it himself. If they ever did anything, she had to say what, how and when, and then afterwards he'd rant and rage about the fact she was domineering, and not a woman or a wife. She said he would ask to be flogged, or restrained and then threaten to report her for abuse. I believe her. It explains so much I didn't understand when I was growing up. Bastard. No wonder she retreated into herself. He's an out and out shit, but at least I can now see why he's such a prick regarding my lifestyle."

"Are you okay with it?" Ailsa asked as Aidan stopped the car outside a door marked with the number one. "And about your mum?"

"Yeah. It explains a lot, I reckon. Poor Mum. She did say now, since she's met the perfect man, she's a switch. It was a bit of an 'oh-ho, too much info, Mum' moment, but then I'd just confirmed what she thought about me, so in the end we're both happy each other is happy, if you get my drift. Right, let's go in and you can spill the beans about everything. I'm itching with curiosity." He made a show of scratching his arms, before he got out of the car to walk round as Ailsa struggled out of her seat.

He stopped her by the simple method of holding her arm. "It's my job and desire to help you, pet. Please wait next time." It was like someone had flipped a switch and a sign saying 'Dom mode' lit up over his head.

"No need. I've been getting in and out of cars by myself for a long while now." She straightened and put her hand over his on her arm, in what she hoped was a gesture he understood to be conciliatory.

Aidan tugged her hair to just the enjoyable side of pain. "I want to."

Ah, now she understood.

"With respect, Aidan." Alisa used his name deliberately and hardened her heart to the cloud she saw in his eyes. "I can't promise I'll always remember. And I'm not accepting the Dom card out of the bedroom so to speak unless we've pre-agreed it. Like now, for instance. In effect, even though I told you I was off duty, for now this is official business. So no Dom/sub unless we reverse our roles." She bent down to the floor of the car and picked up her handbag.

"Point taken, but seeing you like that sure brings the Dom out in me."

Ailsa nodded and let him help her out of the car. She turned around and stood on tiptoe to kiss Aidan on the cheek.

"Good, and please, Sir, hold that thought. For now I need to get my scattered thoughts together and forget all about you, me and subbing. I want to get this sorted as best I can, and then enjoy what's left of the weekend. Well, if you want me for a sub after I've told you all everything?" *Damn, I sound all pathetic and whinging. I'm a bloody police inspector with a job to do. So if he decides his Domming of me is over almost before it's begun, suck it up buttercup.*

Aidan hugged her. "You're not getting out of me scribing you that easily. Come on, let's go in and you can get your confess-fest over and we can drink wine and bitch about arsehole fathers and whatever."

He went to the door and rang the bell.

"They might not want me within a hundred miles of Diomhair once I've told them everything. Nor might you. But this is my job, and it's better I do it than someone unsympathetic to your lifestyle."

Aidan swung her around and gave her two short and hard smacks on her bottom. Even through the linen and her knickers — they were firmly back in place — it hurt.

"Enough already. Stop whining. We're better people than that and you do us all a miscarriage of justice."

The door opened and Jeff stood back to let them in.

"I have a wife who is eaten up with curiosity, a sister blaming herself because she knows you and a mate who hopes Aidan has the balls to show you the error of your ways," he said. "For myself, the jury is out, but if you upset my wife, it sure won't be."

Ailsa took a step back. Okay, she hadn't thought it was going to be a walk in the park, but such out and out antagonism was hard to accept.

"And I don't have a warrant, but I'm sure I could get one for something or other, and a Dom who is backing me one hundred percent." Well, she hoped he was. "Plus a job to do, so thank your lucky stars it was me, who could check for things without exposing everyone and everything to those wolves otherwise known as journos. Because believe me when I say they have contacts everywhere, and seem to get in and out of anything and anywhere like a bloody midge. Swift and unseen. At least I can keep my mouth shut. As can my boss. So it's up to you. I have permission to come and talk to you all, ask for your opinions and such. However..." She shrugged. "If you'd prefer for it to be all official, I can arrange for that, no problem. Then I can dump your problems onto someone else, go away with my Sir and have a great weekend." She looked at Aidan who seemed to be doing his best not to laugh, then at Jeff. "Up to you, Mr Richie."

"Oh, come in." Jeff's tone had no invitation in it whatsoever. "No need to go all official on me. Aidan vouches for you, so we'll give you the benefit of the doubt." He stood back to allow Ailsa and Aidan to enter.

It was a grudging acceptance, but under the circumstances Ailsa didn't think she was badly off. She walked past him and stood to one side.

"After you."

Jeff glared. However, he led the way upstairs.

"You, pet, are pushing your luck. He doesn't lose his temper often, but when he does, we all duck," Aidan said in a low voice as he patted Ailsa's bum to urge her upwards.

"Likewise. I'm trying not to be rude or offensive or officious, but if he carries on that way, I can go exactly by the book. Tedious, time consuming and a lot of paperwork. I've been given the opportunity to, shall we say, tell a few tales out of school, but I don't have to, not if I think it will cause trouble."

"It won't, not if you're honest." Jeff had overheard her. His tone implied that he thought she'd be anything but.

Ailsa bit her lip on the retort she wanted to give. Antagonizing him now wouldn't be a good move. If she upset him later, that was just tough.

"Jeff, you're being a prick," Aidan said in a conversational tone. "Give her a chance, and *then* sound off on one if you see the need. Remember, Ailsa's put her job on the line for you. The least you can do is have the courtesy to listen."

"Eh?" Jeff had the grace to look somewhat ashamed. "Yeah, 'kay. This way."

"If that's consideration, never let me be near him when he's *not* in a considerate mood," Ailsa said as they followed Jeff into a lounge where Jess, Kath and David sat. None of them looked much more welcoming than Jeff had.

Ailsa sighed. It was going to be a long evening. Her tummy rumbled and she took her notebook, pencil and oat bar out.

"No, don't eat it if you can hold on 'til you've talked," Kath said. "There's chili and rice ready for us."

Ailsa obligingly put the bar down. She sighed again and took a deep breath. Aidan winked and sat on a chair as near to her as he could. He tapped his lap. "Want a seat?"

"I wish. Later maybe," she said in a low voice. Then she raised it. "Right so let me introduce myself properly. My name is Ailsa McLagan. I'm a police inspector attached to a special squad who are tasked to do jobs that perhaps are not run of the mill. I met Jess by accident, just after I'd been detailed to try and find out if anything" — she hesitated — "nefarious or illegal was occurring in here. We were tipped off that something illegal *was* happening inside Diomhair. Because I knew the castle from childhood, I was detailed to get inside and see what I could find out." She smiled. "And also, I suspect, to keep my boss out of it. I can tell you now, I saw nothing untoward inside, but why on earth was a white van parked outside that half-ruined cottage set off the drive?"

Jeff shot up out of his chair like a bullet from a rifle. "When?"

Chapter Eleven

"Several times. Once I had to hide whilst it drove along the front drive and out of the back. Why?"

"Someone in a white van knocked Kath over when she was pregnant. It was a woman."

"Well it wasn't me." Alisa stared at Jeff who looked anywhere but at her.

Aidan glared at Jeff, who flushed and sat down again. He had a right to be angry, but truculence directed at Ailsa was a waste of energy.

"I didn't say it was." Jeff ran his hand through his hair, and Aidan could see the worry in his eyes and in his stance. "But happenstance and all that. Breaking in, white vans, someone digging and moving stuff around in the grounds. Then you pop up so conveniently. Well." He shrugged. "Even I can add two and two together."

"And make twenty. Arsehole, do I really have to admit you're my brother?" Jess asked. She was sitting on David's lap and even his pinch to her arm didn't faze her. "Well, listen to him, Sir. He sounds like a dong, not a Dom."

Jeff lifted his shoulders and spread his hands out in supplication. "God, I'm sorry, but this should be a happy time. The club is successful. My sister is accepting what she is. We have two healthy babies, and I'm soon going to be a husband as well as a Master."

"If you stop behaving like a right royal prick you will be," Kath said. "Seriously, Jeff, you should hear yourself. Whine, whinge, woe is me. Grow a pair. Listen to the inspector and then throw the dummy out if you need to, not before."

Aidan loved it. Women power was alive and well, even in the lifestyle.

"Go ahead, Inspector. Ignore those who are talking out of their arse." Kath tugged on Jeff's T-shirt and pulled him back into a seat. "This is where I wish I was a switch, and had a ball gag handy."

Jeff laughed and kissed her. It seemed his good humor was restored. Aidan was glad. He suspected it was going to be hard enough for Ailsa as it was without open hostility.

Ailsa smiled. "Thank you. Right, so to reiterate, we were given a tip-off that the castle was being used for something illegal—nothing specific, but more than likely narcotics. We've known for a long while drugs were coming through this area but not exactly where and how. The tip-off hinted it was here, inside the castle. I was asked to get in and have a look around. Which I did, and found nothing illegal or untoward. I was on the last visit I intended to make when I was busted. Luckily for me, Aidan accepted I was a missing sub. Or decided to give me enough rope to hang myself. When he asked how I wanted to play, I gave in to temptation. Of course, as he told me later, he had no intention of doing anything of the sort, until Ross and Connie reappeared."

"Ah, Connie, the WPC. Is she in on this as well?" Jeff asked. "She was open about her profession, and I'd hate to think it was all for this."

Ailsa shook her head. Aidan noticed that now she was talking about her work, she was calm and confident.

"No, she was as shocked to see me as I was her. I don't know half of the local force, but we'd worked together on a case a fair while ago. The only thing I did do was pull rank over her, and insisted on confidentiality. So, that's it in a nutshell. My boss is now certain that you and the castle are in the clear. We don't know what's going on in the grounds, but with your permission we would like to be around to see. And yes, we probably could have done it without you knowing, but I advised that in this instance you should know. It could be an employee. It could be major. It could be someone burying the proceeds of a wee breaking and entering. We don't know if it's anything to do with our tip-off or not. That's all I know." She leaned against Aidan. He felt the shivers and trembles that she was doing her best to hide.

"Well done, pet. Good girl." He hugged her then cleared his throat. "Over to you now, Jeff. If you want us to leave we will do. If you want us to stay, likewise. And if you don't mind later, we might like to borrow a dungeon for a while."

"Sir." Ailsa's tone was reproachful. It was a measure of her agitation that she had slipped into Dom/sub mode without, it seemed, any hesitation. "Not here, please."

"Pardon, pet? Who's topping from the bottom?"

She bit her lip and to his dismay her eyes were full of tears. "Quack."

Oh shit, fuck and bugger. Aidan noticed the others were staring at them. After a quick look at David, and getting a brief nod, Jess got off David's lap and walked across to them.

"Sir, my Sir says may I take Ailsa with me to get our supper ready?"

Aidan nodded. It was a good way to defuse the situation and maybe Ailsa would confide in Jess and get sub-to-sub guidance. Sometimes Aidan wondered just where a woman's mind went. Mind you, he thought fairly, men weren't a lot better.

"Of course. Okay, pet?"

Ailsa nodded. "Yes, thank you, Sir." Her voice was hardly above a whisper. Where was his confident, in charge Ailsa now? He accepted he'd been in the wrong. She'd said before she wasn't happy scening in public, and how was she to know he'd wanted a dungeon for the two of them to talk in, so he could explain about all the various aspects of the club? To show her what he meant by scribing, but not hurting her, and to perhaps then and only then play a little with or without a Dungeon Master. As friends, each of them could play alone, just like they did at home. Of course maybe they hadn't gotten to that stage, but after their little session earlier, Aidan had hoped they had.

Aidan kissed her cheek. "Trust me, pet. It's maybe not what you think." He wasn't used to explaining himself. Once again Aidan had to remind himself how green Ailsa was with regards to the lifestyle. "Talk your worries over with Jess. Then we can chat. In a dungeon. Alone."

Her eyes widened and she let her head bend downwards. "I've jumped to conclusions, haven't I, Sir?"

"Yes, but I did nothing to help you. We both have a lot to learn. Go on, get my supper, woman." He rubbed his stomach in a way that any actor would be proud of. "Feed my stomach so we can feed my soul later." He patted her bum, not even hard enough to sting.

Ailsa rolled her eyes. "Pitiful. Okay, Sir, gone." She followed Jess to the door, giggling as she went.

Aidan looked at the others. Kath put her fingers in her ears. "I'm deaf. Anyway I need to go and check on the babies. You can go all Dommly and brag amongst yourselves. Give me a hand up, Jeff. I'm rig welted here." The expression used by farmers to say a sheep couldn't get up was one Aidan hadn't heard for ages, but watching Kath trying to get to her feet, it seemed apt. She went out of the room, and the three men looked at each other.

"Apart from the fact we're being cussed from here to the capital and back, and being trashed along with it, what the fuck is going on?" David asked as he poured three whiskies out.

"Not for me, I'm driving," Aidan said.

"Rubbish. We've both got spare rooms. Relax, let your lady relax and understand we're not all whips and chains, and let's try to sort some of this shit out."

* * * *

"Any idea what really is going on? Sub to sub, friend to friend and sod the men?" Jess walked around the kitchen, taking out plates and cutlery as easily as if it was her own flat, not her brother's. "Damn, where does Kath keep the chutney?"

"In the fridge?"

"Yeah, ta. So?"

Ailsa shrugged. "Not a lot. I covered it all, I think."

"Except the bit about a certain high heid yin policeman and his wife being members." Kath came into the room with Grey in her arms. "Lola's still asleep so I've brought him with me so he doesn't wake her up. He forever needs top-ups. Typical male. I do the records."

"Ah well, you've confirmed what I suspected," Ailsa said. "Male wise and everything else. But I didn't know for sure. It was just the way he winked and said Aidan would be good for me that made me wonder."

"And will he be?" Kath latched the baby on, and held him tight. "He's a good man and, I think, a good Dom. We've got to know him well since he began to help out."

"I hope so. I didn't know what I wanted or needed until he showed me. But I do know I don't want or need it in public."

"Why? You scened in front of Ross and Connie, didn't you? What's the difference?" Kath asked as she burped Grey and swapped him to the other nipple. "This one is a snacker, I tell you. Lola now will stay on one side for ages. Not my boy. Sorry, so what *is* the difference?"

"I don't know. Oh grief, it's just the all mixed up learning curve. I don't want people seeing my boobs and going 'Ohh you don't get many of those to the pound'."

"What?" Jess put down the knife she was holding and looked at Ailsa in amazement. "What crap are you spouting now?"

"My boobs. Hell, they grew and I didn't."

Jess shook her head. "For a supposedly intelligent woman you don't half talk a load of bullshit. What are you, 36D? Double D?"

"Double D. But I'm only five feet two."

"And your point is? Lordy, Ailsa, none of us are satisfied with what we've got, but it's how we use it that matters. If your boobs are the perfect handful for your Sir, what else do you need?"

"Ah, but I don't know if they are. Hell, Jess, we've made love once and scened once, that's all."

"Well, think of the fun you can have showing him how they fit him." Jess was unrepentant. "Remember, we, the subs, have the power to make or break the relationship. Don't break it just to see if you can."

Ailsa nodded thoughtfully. Was that what she was doing? She made her mind up.

"If I go in and respectfully ask Aidan to play with me, will you be there for support?"

"Just in there or in the dungeon? Oh you'd better go and say something right away, because I saw Jeff getting whiskey out and offering you both a room for the night."

"In the dungeon. And yes, best do it now before I lose my nerve." Her tummy rumbled again. "At least I can't lose my dinner, I haven't had any."

"Here." Jess handed her a banana. "That'll keep you going."

Ailsa swallowed it in four bites. "Okay, let's do it."

Chapter Twelve

Aidan looked up from the whiskey he hadn't touched as Ailsa entered the room without any food and walked across the carpet toward him. She knelt and assumed the perfect position. Behind her Jess did the same to David.

"I would if I could, but I have Grey so I can't. Consider it done, though," Kath said as she carried her feeding son in with her. She settled in her chair. The only noise was the slurp of a contented baby. It seemed this time he wanted more than a top-up.

Aidan touched Ailsa's shoulder. "Do you want to say something, pet?" Her sensuous perfume, with hints of musk and spices, surrounded her and Aidan guessed it had just been applied. To make her feel good about herself and give her courage?

She looked up at him and swallowed. As ever, the ripple of her muscles called to him in the most primitive way possible and his cock swelled.

"Please, Sir."

"Go on then." Aidan would never call himself fanciful, but he would have said that the air was heavy with expectation.

"Please, Sir. May we play? And have our friends as our audience?"

Whatever he had thought she was going to say, it wasn't that. He set the whiskey down carefully. "In what way, pet?" Out of the corner of his eyes he saw both Jess and Kath watching carefully.

Then David winked at him and Jeff gave a thumbs-up.

"Well, Sir. When I first met you, you asked if I wanted wax or scribing. I've had the wax, so…" Her voice trailed off. Then she cleared her throat. "Will you do me the honor of scribing me, Sir?"

Aidan felt tears come to his eyes. He blinked rapidly at her simple but emotional words.

"Will you do the honor of letting us see if we can have a relationship? Even though our friendship, lovers, Dom/sub life is very new. Are you willing to try?" He'd forgotten the others. His whole being was focused on Ailsa. "Will you let me look after you, be your Sir, within our defined relationship? Help us learn together? One day perhaps be collared and mine, all mine?"

Her eyes were shining, and he reckoned she was as near to tears—hopefully tears of happiness—as he was.

"Yes please, Sir."

Behind her both Jess and Kath sniffed. Aidan looked at David and Jeff and grinned.

"Gentlemen, we have a dungeon to set up. Pets, you have half an hour. Then please present my pet to me in…" He looked at Jeff.

"The green dungeon," Jeff said. "And we'll go with protocol, please."

The three men walked out.

"I don't know what protocol is," Ailsa said. "I'm scared."

"It's nothing awful. No wife or sub swapping and no playing with each other's sub," Jess said as she stood up. "Come on. Kath has to feed and settle the babies before she can even think of joining us. And even then, don't pout, love, you know what I'm going to say is true, she might not be allowed to do more than sit at the back with the baby monitor in her ear. That way if they wake up she won't disturb you if she has to go out. Protocol is clothes and discipline. I'll talk you through it whilst we get changed."

"I've got nothing to change into," Ailsa said as she trailed behind Jess in the direction she knew would take them to the female changing area.

"I bet you have," Jess opened the door and peered inside a locker with its door ajar. "Told you. We have a shop on site, and I thought Aidan would have paid it a visit, just in case. Oh my, this is lovely, look." She took out two items of clothing.

Ailsa looked as she was bidden and burst out laughing. "Well, I know he said he wanted to see me in a leather thong and bustier, but I didn't think it would be quite so soon."

"It's fantastic. If you want privacy to change, there's a wee room over there, but don't mind me." Jess took her top and jeans off so fast, Ailsa blinked. Within a few seconds Jess wore nothing but a tiny, tiny frill of a skirt and a low bra that barely covered her nipples. She must have felt Ailsa's gaze on her.

"Ha, a year ago you wouldn't have got me out of jeans and a top for a king's ransom. Now normally I wouldn't wear the top. But I love David and he loves me, and if he says braless, I'm all for it. Tonight I think it's let's ease Ailsa in gently. But seriously, think about it. What's wrong with topless? After all, we're all built on the same chassis. Well, women are one way and then men are in another. Do you need help?"

"No," Ailsa said slowly. She'd never thought of it quite like that. She took a deep breath—she seemed to be doing that a lot these days—and stripped down to her bra and pants.

"Honey, with the best will in the world, you can't wear a lacy bra and a pair of granny pants under that. Do you wax?"

Ailsa jerked out of her reverie. Was she going to wake up and find this was all a wet dream and she'd need her vibrator?

"Jess, do me a favor. Pinch me."

"Sure."

Jess obliged and Ailsa felt the sharp nip. Not asleep then.

"Okay, yes, I wax. Down to a landing strip anyway. I've never been brave enough to dare to be bare."

"You will. Hurry up we've not got long."

Whether to spare Ailsa's blushes, or because she wanted to tie back her hair using a mirror, Jess walked to the other end of the room. Ailsa stripped her underwear off and pulled on the tiny scrap of leather that fitted where it touched and didn't leave a lot to the imagination. Then she looked at the bustier. She would never get her boobs in that.

"I don't think this is big enough." She pulled it on and held the edges together. "I need another six inches of leather."

"Nah, turn round." Jess loosened some strings and tied the rest over Ailsa's breasts. At least four inches of boob and chest showed in a long strip down the front.

"Stunning. Look." Jess steered Ailsa to a mirror angled beside another one so she could see her front and rear. Apart from the fact that she felt totally exposed, Ailsa decided it looked good. If only she didn't have to let other people see. Her arse was split by a tiny strip of red leather and her back criss-crossed with tiny red leather thongs that highlighted her pale skin.

"Agree?"

Ailsa nodded. "I do."

"Ready?"

"I'm shit scared, excited and worried my bum looks big in this, but yeah, I'm as ready as I'll ever be. Let's do it."

"Shoes. You'll take 'em off at the door, but tonight we wear them to just inside. Here."

Ailsa looked at the red, fuck me heels. "I'll fall over in them."

"Nah, I'll hold onto you." Kath had entered the room, with one ear plugged by an earphone. "As we thought, I'm at the back by the door. I've been sent to get you. And you both look fab. I feel frumpy."

She didn't look it. In her low cut sundress she looked glowing. Ailsa said so.

Kath curtsied. "Thank you, ma'am. Now come *on*."

Ailsa came with Jess bringing up the rear. *To make sure I don't bolt?*

They stopped outside a green door. Kath knocked, waited for the command to enter and stood back.

"You first, Ailsa. Go in, ditch the shoes, go to wherever Aidan is and assume the position. Remember, this is fun. You want it and so does Aidan.

The rest of us are really only here for your safety. Both of you. Oh, and to be jealous. I have three weeks to go and counting."

"Thanks, both of you. Wish me luck and good subbing." Ailsa gave in to temptation and kissed Jess and Kath before she pulled her shoulders back and walked into the dungeon.

Once inside, she closed her eyes briefly to help them adjust to the darker lighting. She slipped her shoes off and wriggled her toes in relief—they nipped—as she located Aidan standing next to a long bed, similar to the one he'd used for his wax play.

With as much grace as she could muster, and not let her hands or legs shake, Ailsa walked over the tiled floor and tried not to gasp at the chill it sent into her feet.

She reached Aidan and suddenly it seemed so natural to kneel at his feet, bow her head and cross her hands behind her back.

The room was silent and Ailsa was sure the others must be able to hear her heart beating.

"Thank you, pet." Aidan tugged her hair. "Look at me." She did so. "Are you ready to be scribed? For me to score your skin and make you mine?"

She swallowed. Put like that, it sounded scary, even though she knew it wouldn't last above a few hours.

"Yes, Sir." Sod it, she did want it, and she wouldn't duck out.

"Then up on the bed and lie on your stomach."

Ailsa did as he asked as elegantly as she knew how. To someone of her height, it wasn't easy to climb up onto the high, long bed, but she managed by standing on tip-toe and grabbing the sides. Once on, she settled on her tummy, and wriggled to get her head positioned over the hole in the mattress. It was just like a massage table.

What I wouldn't do for a massage now.

She felt Aidan's hands on her back, then the two sides of the bustier slipped apart.

It's only your back, nothing else.

"This will sting. Remember, embrace the pain. What's your safe word?"

"Quack, Sir. And I'm g…green."

"G…green." She heard the laugh in his voice.

"Just green, Sir. Ouch." He'd touched her back with something. Either a knife tip or a needle and it stung. Worse than pricking her finger, but not as bad as a paper cut.

"Breathe and embrace the pain."

His voice was even, but held no soothing tone. It commanded obedience and Ailsa responded as she reckoned he expected her to. She began to take deep, even breaths as the stings and pain spread over her back. Then it morphed into pleasure. As if she was above it all, experiencing love and arousal. She floated in that haze of arousal as each sting became pleasure, and warmed her skin.

Her clit throbbed, her pussy was wet and her nipples were hard, tight nubs. It would take so little to climax.

Perhaps Aidan realized it, because his breath was warm on her ear. "Does my pet want to come?"

It was hard to form the words she wanted to use. "Hmmm… Mmmm."

He laughed softly and nipped her ear with his teeth. "Come then." Her arse was slapped twice, hard. Any other time it wouldn't be what she needed but at that moment? It was perfect. Along with Aidan's "Now, come now for me, pet," and the way he stroked her neck, Ailsa let go and came with a scream.

The next thing she knew, she was wrapped in a blanket and cuddled into Aidan, and sobbing her heart out. They were alone.

"Ah, pet. Now then, let it flow, you've just experienced something lots of people never do. My brave, lovely pet."

He stroked her back, kissed her cheek and muttered nonsense until Ailsa hiccoughed and sniffed.

"Here, blow."

He handed her a tissue. She took it and blew her nose.

"Whew, sorry."

"No need to be sorry, pet. You've given me such an honor. Subspace so soon is amazing."

She'd read about that. "That was subspace?"

"I reckon so."

"Wow." Ailsa wriggled around on Aidan's lap and felt his erection dig into her bum. She'd have to see if she could do something about that—later.

"Wow," she said again. "Subspace, eh? It was fantastic. Can I see what you did to me?"

"Of course. I've taken your bustier off, well it fell off when I picked you up, but no one saw you like that, except me."

Ailsa nodded. The way she felt at the moment the whole band of the Scots Dragoon Guards could see and it wouldn't bother her. She stood up and walked across to some angled mirrors.

Across her back was a series of tiny raised red lines. She looked at them carefully, amazed at how pretty it looked. Then she realized it was words.

"Will you be mine?" she spelled them out loud.

"Will you?" Aidan asked.

Ailsa turned and walked back to him. Slowly she knelt and going on instinct, and something she remembered from a book she'd read, bent her head and nuzzled his cock through the soft leather that covered it. She hadn't even noticed he'd changed clothes earlier.

"I will, Sir." She nuzzled him again then giggled. "And can we do it all again, please?"

Epilogue

"Someone tell me what the hell I'm doing, standing by a loch at dawn, wearing next to nothing and hoping the midges realize they should be in bed by now and not biting me?" Ailsa twisted her head to look from Jess to Kath.

"Well, we're dressed—or undressed—the same," Jess pointed out. "We're here at dawn because you said that's when you wanted this to happen, and any tourists who want to walk past, sail by or fly over probably won't be up yet."

That was the problem in Scotland. There was no such thing as trespass.

"Okay, yeah but what if...?" Ailsa was stopped from speaking by the simple, but effective method of Kath's hand over her mouth.

"No, what ifs. You want this, don't you?"

Ailsa nodded.

"You love your Sir, he loves you and this is an affirmation of that love?"

Ailsa nodded again.

"There you are then." Kath removed her hand and patted Ailsa's cheek. "Nothing to worry about."

"But all I have on is an under-the-boob bustier, and a blink-and-you'll-miss-it thong. My boss, his wife and Aidan's mum are out there. They'll see me like this."

"And so do we. See you and look like that. Mind you, have you looked at Aidan's mum? Really looked? Didn't you say she was a switch? I reckon she's come as a sub for solidarity's sake. And your boss and his wife are in full on Dom/sub mode, even if she is in a skirt and top."

"Eh?" Ailsa poked her head through the doorway of the canvas tent she and her friends were in. "Ah...blimey." Aidan's mum, whom she'd met several times over the last month, stood next to an impossibly handsome, tall, dark-haired guy. She wore a long and, Ailsa realized, see-through dress and a collar that sparkled in the rising sun. "Yeah, sub power. Okay, let's do it."

She looked at her two friends and smiled. All three of them had accepted their Doms' decision regarding clothes. All three of them had giggled and decided it was worth a punishment to decorate their boobs and nipples with stick on gems.

Kath and Jess both wore ornate and elegant day collars. Ailsa's neck was bare.

But not for long.

She made her way barefoot across the soft grass to where Aidan was waiting, dressed in her favorite leather trousers and black T-shirt. He smiled as she approached, saw her jeweled boobs and chuckled.

"Is this for me? So you can get a nice spanking later?" He kissed her long and hard until a theatrical cough made him lift his head.

Ailsa knelt in front of him. "Of course, Sir."

"Good." His hand was warm on her head. Ailsa tamped down the butterflies in her tummy. This was it. Something much more important than their wedding, due to take place later in the year. This was their commitment to each other in a deeper, more meaningful way.

Her collaring.

"Ailsa, pet. You are my love, my sub and my life. Will you do me the honor of wearing my collar? Commit to me, and be my partner. Let me be your Dom and you my sub. Wear my collar with pride, and to show the world you belong to me?"

She swallowed and blinked rapidly to get rid of the tears his simple and heartfelt words had brought. They hadn't confided in each other just what their exact words of commitment would be.

"Sir, my Master, the honor is mine. I'll be proud to be yours and wear the evidence of our commitment."

Someone, she thought it was Jess, sniffed and choked on a sob.

"Then, pet, I give you this collar, to show the world you are mine, and to vow to you never to do anything to jeopardize our relationship."

The soft leather was warm on her skin as Aidan buckled it around her neck. They'd chosen it together, a thin strip of leather decorated with tiny turquoises, which was her birthstone, along with a thin silver chain with a padlock and key on it that she could wear as a day collar, without eliciting unwarranted comments.

"Mine," Aidan said and drew her to a standing position.

"Yours, Sir."

Aidan turned to their assembled friends.

"May I present my pet to you? My lovely sub, Ailsa."

She grinned. "Even if I am a bratty sub?"

"Especially if you're a bratty sub. Because you're my bratty sub, and I love you just as you are."

SECRETS
DISPATCHED

Dedication

To Jenny. Thank you for all your hard work.
To everyone who reads my books, thank you for your
support.
And as ever, to Paul.

Chapter One

The flight was long and the woman in the next seat a pain in the arse. Shane thanked every god she'd heard of — and made a mental note that if there was any she hadn't heard of she'd thank them as well — that she was in an aisle seat and had her noise blocking headphones on instead of the ones the airline had given her.

Even though she'd sprung for business class — and in effect she had her own personal space — the woman was a walking, talking annoyance, and much too close. Every time Shane put up the privacy screen — surely an indication that she didn't want to be sociable — the woman pushed it down again and began to make inane comments. She even burbled on about Shane's top and how she would go to the same shop to buy one. As it was a plain white tee, Shane decided the woman talked about any old thing because she was lonely or scared.

For a brief second she did feel a pang of sympathy. Terror was a horrible thing to experience alone. Then the woman asked for a double gin and knocked it back in one go, and Shane's sympathy disappeared as fast as the gin. She remembered she'd noticed her in the lounge, drinking glass after glass of the champagne on offer like a lush in a desert. This had happened both back in Australia and when they'd transferred planes in Hong Kong. Shane heard her tell anyone who would listen she hated to fly.

That wasn't something that bothered Shane. She loved it.

"Would you like a drink, madam?" The cabin crew member smiled at Shane as she offered a selection of beverages.

"Gin and tonic please," the woman in the next seat said, interrupting the girl rather rudely, Shane thought. It seemed the crew member thought the same.

"One moment, madam, I'll get to you when I've served this lady." She turned back to Shane and briefly raised her eyebrows.

"Water, please, I hate being dehydrated, and too much alcohol does that to me."

The other passenger snorted. "Helps me sleep."

Oh if only. Shane took her water and sat back in her seat again. The other passenger took her gin and tonic and looked over at Shane.

"You're only young once, love. Enjoy yourself."

"I do, thank you." Shane did her best to be civil, but also show she wasn't interested in chatting. It didn't work. In the end, after several more exchanges of banalities, Shane did something she'd never thought herself capable of. Total rudeness. She shoved the opaque screen upward and heard it click. Then she said good night very firmly and ignored the injured hiss from the other side. It was that or find a policeman waiting to arrest her as she disembarked, on the charge of causing a disturbance on an aircraft.

That would make my brothers think they were right to worry. I'd never get out without a chaperone ever again.

The drone of the engines should have been enough of a constant background noise to lull Shane to sleep. Usually she was one of those people her mum said could sleep standing up and she never had problems dropping off, even after *that time.* Except now. Maybe it was the thought of what she needed to do, but as she stretched out on her flat bed and tucked the airline blanket around her, Shane couldn't even doze. Her mind jumped from one thought to another like a fly dodging a swatter, and she almost sat up, flicked down the privacy shield and demanded the woman on the other side annoy her once more.

That thought was enough to make her punch the tiny pillow into a heap, wish it was a certain, luckily now deceased man's face, roll onto her side and fall into an uneasy sleep. Her dreams were elusive and she woke up a couple of hours later with gritty eyes and feeling like she'd not slept for a week. Which, she thought with hindsight, wasn't far wrong. It was one thing knowing she needed to go to Scotland and find out for herself how someone was faring, another to actually persuade her brothers she knew what she was doing. Especially as she wasn't really sure she did. Her brothers were more than loving watch dogs. They cared for her. It was only the knowledge of just how much they cared and how they had put their lives on the line on her behalf that kept her from railing against their constant attention.

No wonder she hadn't told them about her trip until it was all booked and paid for. Even then they'd argued the toss and demanded she take one of them with her. It was only when she told them it was something she had to do for herself, to lay the demons to rest and move on that they'd agreed. Albeit with the proviso she keep in touch with one of them at every stage of her journey.

My phone bill is going to be astronomical. Ah well, it should be worth it. I hope.

The fasten seatbelt sign flashed on and off like a demented flea, and the huge aircraft dropped and swayed as it hit turbulence. Never one for enjoying the fairground rides that bounced you up and down, Shane gave up any thought of sleeping and reached for her bottle of water. Why on earth had she chosen February for her trip? Hot as Hades at home and cold as the arctic in Scotland, if the weather forecasts were to be believed. However once she'd been sure where her quarry was and she had enough money to see her comfortably through her trip, Shane hadn't wanted to wait.

So here she was, however many thousands of feet in the air and wondering how the hell her visit would end. She put her headphones back on again and turned on one of the allegedly soothing music channels. Mind numbing and bland.

It could have been a minute or an hour before the seat belt sign flashed off again. Shane had no idea. She'd been so lost in her worst case scenario thoughts and about to scream 'turn around, I've changed my mind'. What if the woman wouldn't speak to her? What if she wanted to sue her brothers or something? Okay, they had actually helped the woman, but who knew how the whole sorry state of affairs had affected her.

I must stop thinking of her as just her. Jess. Jess Sutherland — the woman who her ex-boyfriend had abused after she, Shane, had escaped his clutches. The woman her brothers had found bound and blindfold and subsequently rescued, whilst arranging for the demise of the arsehole they'd both trusted. The woman who'd left Australia and got away from all the furor, whilst Shane had had to brazen it out.

That had been fun – not. Thank heavens for brothers.

She wondered what the woman was really like. She'd seen a very blurry photo on one of the popular social media sites and reckoned she looked sane and sensible and not one to be taken in by a dickhead. But then she'd thought that about herself as well, hadn't she? Pete had taken both of them in. Made them think he was a sane and respected member of the community, albeit with a good dose of kink. Anyone with even the minimal knowledge of the BDSM community would have seen straight through him. Sadly, the only insight Shane had was a few fumbling – and gentle – blindfold and bondage sessions, her own imagination and some hot and sexy books. She'd been a lamb to the slaughter.

The kink hadn't bothered Shane. Truth be told, she rather enjoyed the sweet sting of pain that then morphed into pleasure. Her brothers had accidently introduced her to the lifestyle. She'd seen one of them with a girlfriend bound and blindfolded, his cock in her mouth, and her other brother arse deep in the woman and had had to give herself a large dose of self help afterwards. Later it had occurred to her to wonder why it hadn't either repelled her or scared her to death. Even then she'd know that given the chance, it would be for her.

A few days later, she'd come across one of them wielding a crop on the arse of the same woman, and the other attaching nipple clamps to the woman's pendulous breasts. Instead of being disgusted, she'd known straight away she was interested.

Shane squirmed in her seat. *Stop it now. You've hours to go 'til you get off the plane, and self help in the loo is not the thing to do. Or in the seat for that matter.* However, try as she might, she couldn't help reliving the past in her mind.

When she'd met Pete, Shane had thought she'd found her perfect Sir. Right until that last time when he'd changed into a sadistic, unpleasant and definitely un-Dom-like monster. He'd ignored safe words and all things consensual and had left Shane tied up and blindfold for hours while he jerked off to her pleas to be let free. Until then, she'd wanted to learn more.

For a while she'd closed off her true self, until she was able to believe he was no Dom, just a wannabe and an abuser, and she understood and accepted a true BDSM relationship would be nothing like that. However, over the years she'd lost interest, because there was no one she wanted to please in that way.

Mind you, there had been one guy who she could have subbed for, but as a friend of her brothers and ten years older than her, he hadn't shown any interest in Shane. She didn't even know if he was interested in kink like her brothers, but to Shane's admittedly limited knowledge, he sure looked every inch the Dom. He'd made her pussy wet every time he'd looked at her, even when it was in irritation.

Shane got up and went to the galley for a glass of juice and a chocolate bar. She glanced at her watch — which she'd changed to UK time — and realized they'd be landing in Heathrow in a few hours. Then after the shuttle to Glasgow, she'd need to plot just what she was going to do next. A few hours well spent on the Internet had given her an address for the unknown

Jess — a castle no less. And if her research was correct, one that housed a private BDSM club. It seemed a strange address for someone who'd been abused so badly, but then maybe she was over everything and had rejoined the lifestyle? Whatever. Shane knew she needed to find out for herself. It would be her own completion, one way or another.

Once she'd discovered exactly where the unknown Jess and the castle were, Shane had hired a car and arranged for hotel accommodation not far away. Now she was so close, she didn't want to chicken out.

* * * *

In the end it was surprisingly easy to find where she needed to go. The guy at the car hire had supplied her with a weirdly shaped but surprisingly comfortable and easy to drive car, and assured her it had an integrated sat-nav, which was child's play to program. She wouldn't say that exactly, but by three-thirty she was driving out of the airport on a gloomy and chilly afternoon and along a winding road to her destination. With the heater on high — after all, she'd left thirty-five degrees sun the day before — and the radio blasting out old sixties songs, Shane was almost happy. As long as she ignored the butterflies in her tummy, and the ever present thought of *what if I'm screwing up?*

'At the next junction, turn left.' Sally the sat-nav lady was all bright cheeriness, even when Shane had gone wrong and the tinny, upbeat voice had said *'Ooops, better turn around now'*. This time Shane did as she was bade and ten minutes later, found herself ensconced in a roomy suite in a boutique hotel, which had stunning reviews for its ambience and food. It was a large, old

stone house, overlooking a loch and a mountain and she reckoned the rhododendron-edged drive had been the best part of a mile long. In the summer it would look superb, at this time of the year it just looked gothic and gloomy.

Mist was rolling down the mountain, the loch looked cold and menacing and the sky was dark and heavy. No doubt it was beautiful in the sunshine, but at that moment it showed about as much welcome as you would give to a man in a ladies rest room.

"Snow forecast the morn's morn." The dour old man who'd brought her luggage up on an elaborate trolley essayed a smile, which showed a gap where his front teeth should be. "It's a big bugger, so they say."

Shane nodded as her heartbeat sped up. She'd better get a move on then. She rummaged in her bag to take out an unfamiliar note and handed him a tip. Evidently it was acceptable because he smiled and doffed his tatty tweed cap.

"Thank you, lass. I've to say it's sorry we are for it being me to do this. Lachie, the doorman, is away to the dentist, and he'll be back later." He ambled out of the room. Shane grinned at his quaint phraseology and glanced out of the window.

The weather did look threatening. The color of the sky was a strange gunmetal gray and the clouds low. In the gathering dusk it brought up ideas of strange creatures and ghosts, ghouls and things that went bump in the night.

Stop it now. Shane gave herself a mental shake and poo-pooed her fanciful ideas. After all, it wasn't even Halloween, so she had no excuses for paranormal thoughts. It was around sunset on a late winter's night. Not that there was any sun.

The old man had said snow in the morn's morn. Surely that meant the day after tomorrow? Time therefore to get over her jet lag before she did what she'd come to do. A meal, a bath then an early night with a book and a wee dram, as she'd learned to call a tot of whiskey, sounded perfect.

It was.

Three hours later, at a ridiculously early hour, Shane snuggled under the softest, warmest, duvet she'd ever encountered and switched on her Kindle. This latest BDSM love story was what wet dreams were made of. To say nothing of a juice coated pussy and damp thighs. Plus a need to make herself come. She glanced at her bullet she'd put conveniently on the bedside table and began to read.

The insistent ringing made her jump. That wasn't in the story, surely?

Shane opened her eyes to see weak sunlight edging around the curtains, and the digital display on the bottom of the television saying ten-thirty a.m. She'd slept the clock round and more. She fumbled for the phone and picked up the receiver. Who on earth was it? She'd rung her brothers before she'd fallen asleep and wasn't due to ring them again until that evening.

Well, ask who it is. She didn't get a chance. As soon as she said hello, someone burst into speech.

"Missy, are you wanting breakfast? Service stops at eleven. If you've got that jet lag, you'll be needing food." It was the dentist-going Lachie, who she'd met the evening before, and who, he'd informed her, also worked the desk and the phone. The hotel was small and the staff all multi-tasked when necessary.

"Oh sh—shoot. Please. I'll be down in ten." Shane scrambled out of bed and had the quickest shower on record, before she dressed and dashed downstairs to beat the deadline by just over five minutes. As she thought, the dining room was empty of guests, but a cheery waitress showed no signs of annoyance at a tardy diner. It wasn't long before Shane tucked into a full Scottish breakfast, right down to black pudding and haggis, and washed it down with strong black coffee. She sat back and looked at her empty plate. If she carried on eating that amount every day, she'd need two seats when she flew home.

The promised snow hadn't materialized yet, and mindful of the diktat 'the morn's morn', Shane thought it might well be best to suss out the landscape so to speak, and see if her quarry was at home. She couldn't find a phone number, either for Diomhair Castle or J. Sutherland, and guessed both must be unlisted. Therefore she would need to drive over and see for herself if Jess was around. If she was and they talked, then Shane could come back to the hotel and maybe decamp into the city before the probable storm hit.

"So, what are you up to today then?" The waitress had arrived to clear the table. "If you want to see something of the area, you'd best do it today. There's maps and guidebooks to borrow at the reception desk, and if you don't have a British mobile, we'll lend you one. Too expensive to use a foreign phone all the time. Tomorrow will be a sit in front of the fire and read a book day. The library is the wee room to the left of the front door, if you need something to read. Mind you with thon e-readers, it's easy now isn't it? We've generators and coal fires if the electricity goes down. Oh, don't worry. At this time of year the snow doesn't stand for long, and they have the lines fixed in no time, but tomorrow now? Better not be outside. You could have a spa session or something, eh?"

Shane nodded, somewhat bemused by the flow of information. "I'm going to look at your local castle, I think. It said on the net it'd been restored."

The look on the waitress' face was wary. "It's private."

"I thought there was no law of trespass?" Shane said airily. "I know I won't be allowed inside, but surely I can go and look?"

The waitress—Katrine, her name badge read—looked dubious. "Hmm, Tuesday isn't it? Yes, I reckon you'll be okay to drive up and look. It's close... Er, close by."

Shane would swear Katrine hadn't meant to say close at all. Closed maybe? Did it mean she knew about the club, and it was closed on a Tuesday? Maybe that would make it easier to see Jess and talk to her? Whatever. Shane made her mind up to set off as soon as she could.

"That's great then. I'll go into the village for souvenirs once I'm ready and do my sightseeing. I'll be back in time for dinner, so can you book me a table for seven?" That way, she'd made sure someone knew where she was. Ever since Poisonous Pete the Plonker, as she'd dubbed him eventually, Shane had been extra careful about letting someone know her whereabouts.

She waved a thank you to Katrine and returned to her room. Once she'd seen Jess, she'd feel a whole lot better and be able to move on.

Shane scrambled into her boots and thick coat, borrowed one of the British mobile phones and went outside to the car. By the time she'd driven out of the grounds of the hotel and turned onto the route that sat-nav Sally assured her was the correct way to go, the weak sunshine had turned to a misty drizzle. Within ten minutes it became sleet that covered the road in whiteness and made it incredibly slippery. For one brief moment, Shane wondered if she should turn around and go back to the warmth and safety of the hotel. However, she reckoned she only had a few more miles to go to her destination, and there wasn't anywhere to turn. Not only that, if the weather forecast from the hotel was correct, the next day would be a no go. Best to carry on.

A white van came out of nowhere and sped past her in the opposite direction, spraying muddy slush over her windscreen, which blocked out her view. The car swerved and for one heart-stopping, and she admitted bowel-clenching, moment, Shane was unable to see the road. She swore. The last thing she wanted was to end up in the ditch. She'd have to pay a fortune if the car was damaged, to say nothing of then trying to find her way to the hotel with a broken ankle or something. She drove on slowly but steadily and thanked the fact she'd learned to drive on muddy dirt roads as well as asphalt. Mud or sleet, Shane was of the opinion there was not a lot of difference in the slippery stakes.

However, the one problem with sleet, Shane decided ten minutes later, was that it turned to snow. Heavy fat flakes that rapidly covered the windscreen, which the wipers had a hard time to dispel. Snow wasn't something she encountered very often. By then, she was traveling along a narrow drive, which, according to the now annoyingly cheerful Sally and a tiny discrete plaque on the gatepost, was the entrance to Diomhair, and was a private road — no trespassers. It was irritating to have to get out of the car to brush the snow off to read it, and debate on the wisdom of turning on to it. However, Shane was sure she'd read somewhere that there was no law of trespass in

Scotland, even if Katrine hadn't actually agreed with her when she'd asked the question earlier. Therefore, she ignored that bit as a warning to tourists and itinerant sales people.

Do you even get those these days? Isn't it all telephone calls and spam emails? She was somewhat hazy on the subject and after all, this was Scotland, not Australia. How was the net around here? Her phone, as well as the one she'd borrowed from the hotel, was hovering on one bar of reception, and the radio in the car delivered very little music and almost total static.

Shane rounded a bend with care and was relieved she had done so when the back of the car fishtailed and slid into a skid. She drove into the skid with competence and corrected it. She wasn't an outback girl for nothing, even if she did live in the city now.

Ahead, almost hidden in the gloom, she could just make out a tall, dark stone building with a turret.

A turret? Wow. It was a real castle it seemed and not some mock Victorian monstrosity. Shane hadn't had time to research the history or even if this Jess lived in it as her private home. Was it one house or apartments? Was it offices and a health club as well? Whatever it was, it was big and imposing and austere against the white of the snow. Shane fell in love with it there and then. How fantastic to live in it in any way.

The brief information she'd found on the net had been vague in the extreme. The car lurched over some unseen object, well hidden in the snow, and Shane brought her mind back to the alleged roadway. Wool gathering wasn't a good idea in that sort of weather. She realized she was probably driving over the verge and not on the tarmac surface. If it was even tarmac, she had no way of knowing.

With hindsight she regretted setting off from the hotel without bringing an insulated mug of tea or one of the delicious looking cookies she'd spied to sustain her. Even though she'd had that big breakfast not long before, her tummy rumbled and her mouth was dry. Apprehension or excitement? A bit of both probably.

Nevertheless, by the time she pulled up outside a big wooden door, she was shaking and it wasn't all down to the weather and lack of food. She decided she was scared. Scared that Jess might not be there, scared she was. Scared that Jess would hate her, not be prepared to talk and leave Shane unable to find completion. Shane switched off the engine, and watched the snow fall. It better slow down soon, or she'd be hiking back. Was it quicker cross country? How dare the snow defy the weathermen and come a day too soon?

Wuss, get out of the car. Or turn on the engine and go away for good and try to enjoy a cold, wet holiday. She took a deep breath, did her coat up, pulled her hood over her head and stepped out of the vehicle. A blast of icy wind rocked her on her heels and almost took her breath away. The temperature had dropped considerably, and the snow was now so heavy her tire tracks were almost obliterated.

Shane hoped to hell someone was at home, or she'd more than likely be found in spring as a frozen corpse inside her buried car. She moved toward the castle door with her breath making white, misty spirals in the air and with snowflakes on her eyelashes. Thank goodness for contact lenses. Specs would be useless. Mind you, she patted her pocket to make sure her lenses case and her glasses were there. She'd lost too many lenses in the past and ended up half blind, not to carry specs around, annoying though it might be.

She looked at the walls of the castle and groaned. She had to get in there? Why not try something less challenging like breaking into the Royal Mint or wrestling with a croc.

Okay you can do it. Deep breath and go.

The snow was piled up higher near those forbidding walls and even though she only had a few yards to trudge through it, her jeans were soaked by the time she searched for the doorbell. To her amusement, it was an old fashioned tug rope type. Not that she felt much amused. Pissed, more like. Could they not have an ordinary bell like everyone else? It would take a giant to get a good sound from it, not a five foot something woman.

She hauled and after a second or two, heard a deep clang echo inside the building.

"Come on. Hurry up." Shane pulled the bell again. "Please, please someone answer the bloody door." She stamped her feet, to try and get her circulation moving faster and for the first time thought what an idiot she'd been to continue her journey to the castle once the snow started. Shane dipped her head to pull her hood farther over her head in a vain effort to keep her hair dry. Already frizz-head hair had begun, and she'd have a devil of a job with it once she got it dried again. Not for the first time, Shane wished she'd kept it short in the style she'd cut it after the arsehole experience, as she now called it. Instead, she'd let it grow, more as a way to show herself that Poisonous Pete the Plonker and his only long hair is acceptable diktat, wasn't why it was long. The one thing she did do now—which he'd objected to—was using straighteners on it. Hence knowing that all her hard work was about to be ruined if no one answered the door.

"For fuck sake, open won't you? What if I say open sesame? Or get on my knees and beg? Will that work?"

There was a grating noise, and a blast of heat hit her. Before Shane looked up, someone spoke.

"Open sesame won't. But I do like the idea of you on your knees and begging. I won't make you do it in the snow though."

Oh, fuck and shit. I know that voice.

Chapter Two

Ross Mackie looked down at the snow-covered woman in front of him and wondered if he was hallucinating. Who in their right mind would be out and about this far from a semi-decent road in weather like this? Especially with her head bowed and if you discounted the fact she wasn't on her knees, in an almost perfect subbie pose.

Was this some kind of joke? Had Jeff and David decided to teach him a lesson for refusing to go on holiday and, as they said it, recharge his batteries? The only place Ross knew how to do that was right there, at Diomhair with the perfect sub. Not on a far-flung beach or on a city break bored out of his skull, all by himself.

Sadly he'd come to the conclusion there was no such thing as a perfect sub, at least not for him. Seeing his colleagues all loved — and subbed — up brought it home very forcibly that he had no one in mind to play with on a permanent or even semi-permanent basis.

Goodness knows why. There were plenty of people who were members of the club who would go down on their knees for him to practice his area of expertise on them, but none he would choose to do so with. Except on a teaching basis. For a while, he'd thought he and Connie, one of the subs, would make a go of it, but eventually they'd both agreed they made better friends than Dom and sub. She still subbed for him if he needed one for a demonstration, but that was it. By choice or not, he was alone.

Sad or what?

Now his interest and his cock were piqued. It was a shame it was so bloody cold, because he reckoned his dick would snap in half if it got as hard as he sensed it could.

"So, pet? Are you stopping there to become a snowman or do you want to come in? You can kneel and beg inside instead of out here."

The woman looked up at him and scowled. Something about her seemed familiar, but he couldn't put his finger on what. Dark hazel eyes, fringed with long, snow-edged lashes sparked fire at him.

"Ha, ha funny — not. I'm looking for Jess Sutherland. Could I speak to her, please?"

The accent was definitely Australian and very similar to his own. Ross took a step back and gestured. "She doesn't live here anymore."

His visitor went pale and swayed. Ross hoped to hell she wasn't going to faint on him. He might have done his basic first aid training, but swooning women and no one else about was an assault charge waiting to happen. In all honesty, he was probably all kinds of a fool to even think about offering her the option to wait inside until the snow stopped, or Jess turned up. He'd spoken the truth when he'd said Jess didn't live in the castle any more. However, Jess and her husband David had said earlier they were on their way back from Glasgow, and Ross knew Jess and David would call in — snow permitting — on their way to their new home half a mile away.

Ever since Jess had looked in his fridge and seen a moldy orange, two cartons of yoghurt and nothing else, Jess was convinced he was incapable of feeding himself. It didn't matter how much he protested he was about to go to the supermarket, Jess insisted on stocking his fridge and checking he'd eaten the contents.

He took hold of the swaying woman by the arm and held her steady. As he doubted she would be able to turn her car around and drive back down the lane anyway, he really had no option except to offer hospitality. Once he had her safely seated in a chair, he would phone and warn Jess she had a visitor.

The car was parked — or should that be abandoned — in the middle of the flowerbed, albeit a snow-covered one. Ross wondered how she'd managed to even get it that far. The tiny runaround certainly wasn't fit for the weather. Ross didn't want to be accused of letting her drive away and into a ditch.

"Hey, no fainting. Women are only allowed to lose consciousness around me for other reasons, not the weather or lack of someone to visit."

He hadn't meant to say that, especially about passing out, but once said, he couldn't rescind his words.

Those expressive eyes widened, and she almost smiled.

"I can believe that."

Now why did he not think that was what she had intended to say that? What did she mean by it? "Pardon?"

She dropped her gaze, all subbie correctness. Did she even know she exhibited all those traits?

"D'you want to come in and wait for her? She'll pop in soon." Why was he so insistent? After all, he was alone, it was a BDSM club, even if it was closed, and although she looked familiar, he didn't know who she was or what she wanted. Not really a good situation.

"Yes, please, I'll wait. I do need to see Jess. Don't let me stop you from doing whatever you were doing."

Ross stiffened. Talk about a brush off the first order. It was as well she wasn't his sub. She'd not be able to sit comfortably for a week if that was her attitude.

"Follow me." He spun on his heel and walked back along the corridor without waiting to see if she followed it not. The heavy thump as the door closed made him smile. Miss whoever she was had a temper then.

Ross stopped and turned around to look at her. She'd pulled her hood right down and her hair twisted in a mass of dark brown curls over her shoulders. Once again an elusive memory tugged at the edges of his mind. Perhaps if he didn't try to recall who she was, her name would come to him? "Do you realize how stupid you are coming inside when you don't know me from Adam? I could be an ax murderer."

"Are you?" she said and grinned. "I've got a black belt in judo and know how to disarm an ax wielding madman at five paces."

Somehow he doubted it, but he admired her grit.

She waved one hand in the air. "My brothers taught me. They said it works every time."

The cheeky expression on her face made him jump. *Who* was it she reminded him of?

"Ah, good. What's their chosen method of disablement?"

She giggled. "Whip up my top, wave my boobs and when they're gobsmacked, kick them in the goolies and run like hell."

Ross looked down to where her heavy jacket covered her breasts. "I guess that might work."

She nodded. "According to Troy and Jase, it will. I trust them."

Ross narrowed his eyes. The names coupled together like that were as familiar as his own. Rather than ask her to clarify her statement, he chose to prod a little more. It was the most fun he'd had for ages. If she was related to the Donoghue brothers, she knew more about his lifestyle than she let on. He wished he could recall her name. Something not usual, he thought – a boy's name maybe? She'd be around ten or twelve years younger than him, and someone he remembered as a leggy, flat-chested school girl. No wonder he couldn't place her. This woman might still be leggy, but she certainly wasn't flat-chested. Now she was a beautiful and voluptuous woman who piqued his interest.

He'd heard about her accidental voyeur sessions all those years ago. Or was it accidental? He hadn't caught up with Troy and Jase for years. Maybe once she owned up to who she was, he could ask her how they were. For now though...

"I think, girl, you need to explain further. What's your name?" He barked out the question in a short staccato burst of words and she jumped. However, it seemed she wasn't intimidated easily.

She returned his stare with one of her own.

"Why?"

Ross blinked and the pulse in his wrist jumped. One thing he wasn't used to was backchat from sassy subs. He was more used to instant obedience and awkwardly, sometimes blind, adoration. Oh, he liked a bit of spunk, not lap dog placidness, but he never received, or welcomed, such blatant confrontations. They caused more trouble than the excitement the results gave him.

"Just answer the question."

She bit her lip. Not in a worried way, he decided, but more in a considering one. Even though his temper was provoked, Ross had to stop himself laughing. She was so unafraid, and really she should be quaking in her sheepskin boots. There she was with a strange guy, with no one else around, and she was challenging him. *Okay, sunshine, you want it, then by God, you'll get it.*

"You're treading on thin ice, kitten."

Her eyes widened at the sobriquet, and he would have sworn she twitched and began to dip her head before she straightened. "Yeah, true enough. I'm trading words with an arsehole. I'll go and wait in the car."

Ross grabbed her arm as she began to walk away.

"I don't think so. Shit, woman, you'd freeze to death."

"Do not grab me, mate."

She swung her other arm so fast that Ross only just managed to move to one side and miss the fist she shot toward him. Something glinted between her thumb and forefinger and he realized it was a set of keys with the business end sticking out far enough to disable any attacker for enough time to enable her to leave the scene. He took hold of that arm as well, and with difficulty, pried the keys out of her hand. They dropped to the floor with a metallic thunk.

If looks could kill, he'd be six feet underground. She had guts, he'd give her that, but, oh, how stupid to go head to head with a guy who was a good twelve inches taller and several stones heavier. He tamped down his temper. He'd show her how to defend herself properly, later — if she gave him the chance.

Ross held both her hands in one of his and lifted his arm so she had to stand on the balls of her feet. Even that didn't seem to faze her because she tried to twist and kick out. He pulled her even higher until only the toe edge of her boots touched the floor. She lifted one booted foot, balanced on the other and tried to knee him in the balls. Ross moved until her back was against the wall and put his own leg across her, so she had no room to maneuver. He pressed hard enough for her to wince and gasp. It served her right. Not only for being arsy but also for being so bloody stupid to first of all come in and afterwards to carry on in the way she had. Did she have a death wish?

"Naughty. But at least you've woken up to the danger of being alone with someone you don't know."

"Not really."

Ross waited for her to continue. She looked very pointedly at his hand, which he still had clamped tightly around her arm.

"You haven't?"

Surely she was kidding him. However, she didn't look as if she were joking. More that she knew something he didn't. Ross wasn't very happy about that.

She firmed her lips. "Nope. Now let me down."

"Not a chance, kitten. Silly subbies need showing the errors of their ways." Why on earth was he insisting she was a sub? And calling her kitten? He never, ever used a special nickname for a sub. It was always pet. Apart from which, she probably didn't even know what he was talking about.

"Tell me about it," she said, somewhat cryptically, he thought. "But as I'm not a silly subbie, you can let me down."

"Hmm." *So she does know then.* Life was beginning to get interesting. He stared at her and she stared back. This close, her scent drifted across to him to tease his nostrils.

"Jo Malone?" he asked.

"No, that's not me." She winked.

"Funny girl. The perfume as well, you know." Ross shook her. It was handy being a full foot taller. It didn't seem to faze her one jot. She waited until he stopped and huffed. Chestnut curls spiraled around her face and she blew a few strands off her nose.

"Need to get this mop trimmed. It's Blackberry and Bay—the perfume, not my hair. Fancy you knowing your perfumes. In touch with our female side now, are we? Bit of a change from footie." She chuckled. "Poor, Ross, you might have me up on my toes, but you're the one at the disadvantage, aren't you?"

"You think so?" *What the hell is her name?* It was years since he'd seen or corresponded with the Donoghue brothers, and they'd played footie and chased subs together. Since he'd left Australia, in fact. "So maybe you should enlighten me."

"Why?"

"God almighty, you'd try the patience of a saint. I'm no saint. Sadist, maybe, but saint? Not a chance."

She swallowed and for one second he thought she'd give in. He was wrong.

"Sadist as in how?" She twisted her shoulders and looked directly at his face. This close he could see tiny flecks of silver in her eyes, and notice just how long her lashes were. "Do you pull the wings off of flies or torture stray cats?"

"No, just torture stray subs."

"Ah…" She was silent for a second. "But if you're a sadist, and this is a BDSM club, then by my reckoning, that makes you a Dom. Therefore you'd follow safe, sane and consensual. Let me say here and now, Ross Mackie, I'm no masochist, and I'd shout red at the top of my lungs if you so much as laid a non-consensual finger on me."

He dropped her back onto her feet so suddenly that Shane swayed and grabbed hold of his arm to stabilize herself. It was that or land in a heap at his feet, and not in the way she reckoned he'd prefer.

Ross Mackie. The guy she'd dreamed of, drooled over and worshiped from afar. With hindsight, it made sense that he was a Dom. Shane had recognized his look of authority even before she'd understood what it meant. He'd appeared in many of her 'tied up by baddies, rescued by the hero' daydreams in her teens — always as the tall dark and impossibly handsome surfer-dude, who saved her from what she and her friends had called a fate worse than death. Of course none of them had really known what that meant, but they'd done a lot of giggling and wondering just what people got up to behind closed doors.

When she'd found out, Shane has been somewhat disappointed. Until she'd seen her brothers then indulged in a little subbing herself. Just as she'd discovered what her preferences were, Pete the

Plonker had upset everything. Since then, she'd had no inclination to dip her toes in the lifestyle pool again. Until now, maybe?

Shane gave herself a mental talking to. He still didn't know who she was, and if he seriously was a sadist, could she cope? It was one thing about dreaming that he spanked her for disobeying her brothers and another to actually let him. The problem wasn't the spanking or anything else she knew about BDSM. It was the sadistic part she wasn't sure about. She'd never really tested her pain threshold and wasn't sure she was ready to do it now. With Pete the Plonker it had been more mental torture he'd enjoyed and she'd gotten away from him before he'd had a chance to be too overly creative.

"Cry red? Would you, now?" Ross asked her in a skeptical voice, as he returned to her last comments. "Because I've got a feeling, kitten, you'd like nothing more than to feel my hand on your bare arse and making it the color of your other cheeks."

She put her hand to her heated face. Damn him, he was right. Her thong was damp and creeping up her arse like it wanted to part the globes in readiness for anything Ross wanted to do.

Don't I get a say in the matter? What's with the pretend I'm a cheese grater not a thong scenario? For fuck's sake. There was no way she could remove the string of her thong without making it abundantly clear what she was doing.

"Bugger you, Ross. Stop it now."

He grabbed her chin and squeezed the soft flesh, just short of inflicting real pain.

"Now listen well, kitten. For whatever reason you're here for, I'm not tolerating language more suited to the gutter. You say your brothers taught you to defend yourself. Did they teach you to be crude as well?"

Boy, is he up his own arse or what?

"Eh? Grief, Ross, you're Aussie." Her voice rose and she strove to lower it. "That's not crude, it's a pleasantry. Get out of yourself and come down to the level of us lesser mortals." His fingers tightened. Shane bit her lip. It was more than likely she'd have a bruise there tomorrow and it hurt, so why was her skin tingling and the darts of pleasure bombarding her making her even wetter? "Sir."

He snorted and let go of her chin. Instead of relief, Shane felt she'd lost something special.

"Look, I'm sorry, but you do seem familiar, and I do know two brothers called Troy and Jase, but their sister was only..." He stopped speaking and tucked his hands into the pockets of his jeans. His action stretched the material over his thighs and cock, which was defined clearly under the dark blue denim. It seemed their interaction had pleased him as much as it had her.

"Was only...?" Shane prompted.

"Was only a kid. And that's one thing you're not."

She nodded. "You're right there. I'm no kid. I'm a grown up with a mind of her own. Who needs to speak to Jess Sutherland."

"Who isn't here. So what do you want to do now, kitten?"

"Not be called stupid names."

Chapter Three

Why the hell couldn't he recall her name? He remembered her now. A dark-haired virago who'd stared at him all the time as if he were the answer to everything. Did she still think that? So far it didn't seem likely, but Ross would sure as hell like to find out.

"So, I'll need to be reminded of your name, kitten. Sister to Jase and Troy, known I seem to remember, as pest." That much was true. Perhaps that was why he couldn't think of her name. It was rarely used. "Who used to dog our every footstep, and I'm damned sure nicked a crop of Troy's and used it for riding her horse and goodness knows what else. Why do you need to see Jess?"

She sighed. "It had been my crop in the first place. He took it off me for" — she rolled her eyes — "well, he said because I was messing with it. I reckon he was just being a cheapskate and not wanting to splash the cash and buy one for his own use. Troy never was one for spending if he could manage somehow. My name is Shane. I'm sorry, Ross, I can't tell you why I want to speak to Jess. It's private."

The way she spoke was enough to tell him he'd get no further with his questions. It was a pity because he'd love to know what she meant by messing with it. Ross decided to change the subject and his tactics. After all, he wanted to see what sort of sub she was. Now was his chance.

"Then how about I show you round until Jess gets here?"

She bit her lip.

Ross used his finger to release the soft, red skin from her teeth. "Don't do that, kitten. Any marks will be mine." He winced inwardly as she drew in a deep breath. How presumptuous was that statement? He opened his mouth to apologize, but she broke into hurried speech.

"Why do you say that? Call me kitten and stuff? I've told you I don't like it."

He considered how best to reply. Honestly, of course. Nevertheless, he didn't want to scare her.

"It pleases me," he said at last. "Shane, how much about BDSM do you know?" He took her arm and tucked it in his as he urged her down the corridor. "Not what you sneaked a peek at when you were younger, but really know." He waited as she stared at him.

"A bit." She blushed and twiddled with the edge of her cuffs.

"Here, let's hang your coat up." He'd return to the subject of her knowledge before long. "Or as they say over here, you won't feel the benefit later."

She giggled. "Not much need in Freo."

"True." Fremantle in Western Australia was a lot hotter than winter in Scotland. "BDSM?" he prompted her. "You don't seem uninterested."

"What makes you think that?"

"Oh, come on, kitten. You didn't flinch when I mentioned it. I know for a fact you spied on your brothers at times, and were not appalled or disgusted. You display perfect subbie behavior."

"I do? Shit."

The look of astonishment on her face was so comical Ross burst out laughing. "Apart from the language, kitten. I'd wash your mouth out for that if you were mine."

"Just as well I'm not then."

Bloody hell, you will be.

"Well? What's it to be?" He cursed the impatience in his voice, but he needed to know if it was to be a coffee in the restaurant or a chance to see what appealed to her. He found himself hoping it was the latter. Surely she knew what she was? Or was she one of those people who ignored what stared them in the face? Apart from that, he wondered why it mattered so much to him. He'd been coasting along quite happily, and now out of the blue, someone he thought was a perfect sub attracted him. Sadly she was someone he couldn't play with on a casual basis, not when he remembered who her family was. Ross was honest enough to accept his interest might not be returned, or they might not mesh. Could he take the risk, and face up to the fact there was the possibility of upsetting two of his oldest friends if things didn't work out? He reined in his thoughts. She hadn't even said she was tempted to look around, let alone anything else. He was getting ahead of himself,

"I said, yes, please."

"Ah." He'd been so caught up in his thoughts, he'd missed what she was saying yes to. "Good. Sorry, I was wool gathering." He'd always been one to own up to any shortcoming. "Yes to coffee or…?"

"Both, but coffee first, please. I'm shivering, and my teeth are chattering."

Even in the centrally heated warmth of the castle, her body shook, and he could tell it wasn't from arousal. Ross swore under his breath. "I'll get you a subbie blanket to wrap around you, and take you to my flat. Are you okay with that, or do you want to do your 'here I am' call first?"

Shane grinned, even as her teeth rattled against each other. "I did that while you were, er, wool gathering. Jase says hi, and remember who my brothers are."

As if I'm likely to forget.

Ross nodded, but decided any reply would be inadequate. Instead, he opened a door to their right. "Store room. Give me a sec." He went in and grabbed a new blanket still in its packaging. "Take that coat off and let's get you warm. There's a changing room over there with a shower in it. Do you want to use it?"

Shane shook her head as she handed him her coat and wrapped the soft fuzzy blanket around her body. "No thanks, a cuppa and a nosy around will do fine. Er, when do you expect Jess?"

"No idea." Ross made his mind up. "Look, as we do know each other, sort of, even if it's been years since we met and we both could be ax murders for all we know, *will* you come into the flat? I live here for the time being, and it's a lot warmer and comfier than going to the bar area. The club is closed on a Tuesday." A thought struck him. "You do know what sort of club it is, don't you?" After all, even though they'd been talking about BDSM, had either of them actually mentioned what Diomhair was?

"Yes, and yes. I do my research, you know. Anyway, it's one reason why I need to speak... Oh, shit, ignore that." She shook her head, and he swore he heard her mutter brain addled, under her breath. "Um, which way?"

He let her comment go. There would be time for questioning later. Once he got her reaction to the club and its contents. "This way. We'll use the internal stairs." He led Shane along the corridor and away from the public area. Eventually, in the bowels of the building as Jess once had told him, he stopped in front of a pale gray, anonymous and unmarked door with a fingerprint recognition pad next to it. Ross swiped his finger across it and opened the door to reveal a lift.

"Only goes to the flats," he said. "Mine and the spare one. They used to be for Jess and David and Kath and Jeff—Jeff and Jess are co-owners—but they've built houses on the grounds. I was glad to be given one of these when my lease ran out in town."

Shane went pale. "You really meant it when you said she doesn't live here? Er, damn, I thought you were just being arsy. So will she even come here?"

"If they get back from town." Ross pressed the button to move the lift upwards and leaned on the wall. "Last time I looked, it seemed to be getting bad out there. They might not make it back."

He watched Shane via the mirrored wall as she interlaced her fingers together and moved them to enable herself to nibble on a fingernail.

"You might be stuck here."

"And I might not."

"True. It's in the lap of the gods, I guess."

He was sure she swore and said 'bloody gods', as the lift stopped and they got out.

"Welcome to my humble abode." Ross swung open the door marked with a simple '2'. "*Chez* Mackie."

Shane walked past him and into the lounge. The flat was simply furnished and he knew it had nothing of him stamped on it. It was supposed to be a stop-gap, but six months on, he accepted how much he preferred it to the one he had lived in previously. Maybe it was time to stop roaming and put down some roots? Add a picture or two, or a vase of flowers.

"It's a bit bare," Shane said, confirming his thoughts. "Are you sure you live here?"

"Yeah, and it sure is. It was supposed to be only 'til I got a new flat in Glasgow. Then I realized how much I like living out here. There's no sea like there is at home, but rivers, lochs and mountains are as good."

"I guess," Shane said in a doubtful voice as she went to the window and rubbed a circle in the condensation there. Even with double glazing, it had steamed up a little. "But you can't surf on Loch Lomond."

"True, but I waterski."

"Better than nothing then. Still, I reckon there's plenty of wet stuff today though. It's still snowing." She wriggled her shoulders.

The subbie blanket slid over them, and Ross moved swiftly to set it tighter around her. He peered past her and looked out at the monochrome landscape. From this angle, the trees were stunted, white tipped shapes and the difference between the sky and the land an indistinct blur. Snow was falling steadily, with no indication of stopping, and as the day moved on toward dusk, the light was even more abnormal than he'd ever seen. A storm was in the offing, and he knew for certain there would be no way of Shane leaving any time soon. He wasn't sure if that thought pleased him or not.

"Look, Shane, whatever you want to hope or believe, this weather is set in for the day. Where are you staying?"

"The hotel in the village."

"I think maybe you'd best ring Elspeth at the hotel and tell her you're here with me. Otherwise she'll be calling for the mountain rescue to hunt for you." He pulled the shutters over the chilly scene outside and put his hand in the hollow at the base of her spine to urge her toward the settee. "Mind you, it'd be an easy shout."

"It would?" Shane looked back at him. "How come?"

"I'm one of the people she'd call to go out and hunt."

Shane giggled. "Cover yourself in glory, eh? Are you sure?"

He deliberately chose to misunderstand. "That she'd call me? Oh, yeah."

"No, you moron, that I'll not get back later. I mean, I don't even have a toothbrush with me, let alone a change of clothes."

She sat on the settee and stretched her legs out in front of her. Even though they were clad in damp denim and sheepskin boots, Ross admired the long elegant shape. His cock stirred as he thought of how he'd like to tug off Shane's boots and peel her jeans slowly downwards until her soft skin was bared for him. Of course he didn't *know* her skin would be soft and strokeable, but he'd bet his Firewire surfboard it would be.

"Toothbrush is no problem. We always have new ones in the club shop. Clothes we can cope with. I'll wash and dry what you're wearing and lend you sweats or something for now." He raised one eyebrow. "Of course, we do sell clothes in the shop as well."

Shane shook her head and sighed. "I bet you do. Okay, let me ring the hotel." The call took seconds, and Elspeth, the owner, was pleased she'd called.

"Otherwise, I would have worried," Elspeth said, cheerfully. She didn't sound very worried, just the opposite. "We'll see you when we see you then. Ross will look after you." Was there something in the way Elspeth said it that made Shane sure Elspeth knew exactly who Ross was and what went on at Diomhair? It was probably an open secret to the locals, whatever their preferences were, but she wasn't going to ask.

"Okay?" Ross asked her.

"She was glad I rang, and said you'd look after me?" She ended the sentence on an up note. Shane went back to his last statement.

Ross grinned. "That I will. So, clothes?"

"I can imagine what you sell in the shop." Shane shook her head and sighed. "Joggers or a bathrobe will be fine. No way am I spending the evening in a corset. Bloody uncomfortable, and so not me. My boobs and I need space to expand." She blushed and sniggered. "Shit, that sounds even more kinky than kinky — or weird. Expanding boobs. The mind boggles. Hell, you know what I mean."

"I'd've known what you mean without the cussing, kitten." He used the subbie name on purpose to see how she'd react. To his amusement her lips firmed and her eyes glittered, but she didn't speak.

"Why do you not like the fact I want to call you kitten? It's better than 'hey, you', or 'you, girl', surely?" He sat down next to her and looked at her steadily. "Now's the time to 'fess up, *kitten*. Let's be open and honest, eh? I'm going to grab you something to wear, and point you to the shower." He put his hand over her lips, and felt her breath on his palm as she opened and shut her mouth again. "Good girl. You might say you don't want a shower, but, babe, you're cold and it will warm you up."

"Sheesh, I hate babe even more than pet or kitten. Why can't you call me Shane?"

Ross stood up. "I'll tell you what? You tell me why you hate a pet name, and I don't mean as in animal pet, and I'll not call you kitten — *if* your explanation is justified."

She scratched her nose.

That telling gesture enchanted him. He remembered it as something she'd done as a kid, when she was thinking hard.

"Who's to say if what *you* think isn't justified, *I* do?"

"Well, kitten, that's up to you to decide, isn't it? But you give me good reason not to have a name for us when we scene, and I'll abide by it." He ignored her startled gasp and the way her mouth hung open, until she shut it with an audible snap. "Now, the bathroom is the spare room en suite and it's the third door along the corridor over there. I'm going to make coffee and hunt out something for dinner."

He tugged Shane to her feet and deliberately removed the blanket. He had to pry her fingers open and he chuckled. "I'm a Dom, kitten, cry red or do as I say." He put the blanket over the back of the sofa. "Remember that."

"You're not *my* Dom though, Ross Mackie." She glared at him. She sure did have a good selection of glares and used them to full effect. "So, no dice, mate.

I will have a shower, but only because I want one. Get it?"

He got it. She was arsy and running scared. However, not scared as in frightened, he was sure of that. Scared of her feelings, more likely.

Her chest heaved. It could be with indignation, but Ross saw the way her skin bloomed with a soft covering of perspiration—not dampness from the snow, not now—and how the pulse at the base of her neck beat erratically. He was experienced enough to notice those signs as indicative of arousal not fear. Although were they not different sides of the same coin at times?

"I get it, but I wonder if you do?" Ross asked her. He spun her around to face the direction she needed and patted her bum. "Off you go. Coffee will be waiting when you come back. I'll put clothes on the bed for you."

"No corsets," she said as she sashayed away from him.

Did she waggle her arse like that on purpose, just to tease him, or was it natural? Ross had very mixed thoughts about that, until as she opened the door to the corridor she waved her fingers over her head and, he swore, giggled in an incredibly suggestive way.

Minx. Did she not know little subbies who played with fire got their fingers scorched, and their arses tanned? Or did she not care?

Chapter Four

Shit, shit stupid or what? Do I have a death wish?
Remember Pete. However, Shane knew Ross was a
different kettle of fish to Pete, and understood
whatever she did with Ross would be poles apart
from that earlier negative and unhappy experience.
The problem was whether she wanted it or not. She
accepted she did still have subbie tendencies, and
Ross could well be the Dom for her, but was that
really what she wanted right now? No, she decided,
not until she sorted her past out.

The bedroom she walked into made her whistle. As
a spare room, it was bigger than both her bedrooms at
home put together, and a hell of a lot more opulent.
Not ostentatious, but definitely decorated with a
female in mind. That thought sent a nasty stab of
unwarranted jealousy through her. What right had she
to be jealous of anything Ross had done? Or indeed
still did?

Lots, if he's got someone else. That idea made her feel
sick. Surely he wouldn't have, not if he was interested
in her? Perhaps in being her Dom? That idea made her

pussy tingle and her thighs get damper than they already were.

Pete, you're almost history now. Dead, dead and almost buried.

But, she mused as she kicked off her boots and undid the snap on her jeans, what *did* Ross truly want? Was he just being friendly in offering to show her around, or was it a prelude to asking her to sub? Shane knew without a doubt she needed to know there and then. Without bothering to put her boots back on, she retraced her steps to the lounge and headed in the direction of music. Surely that would be where Ross was?

She was correct. The music got louder as Shane approached a half open door at the rear of the long lounge. She pushed it open to see Ross, back toward her, standing by a work surface, singing along – rather tunefully it had to be said – to an old Bob Marley and the Wailers song. It seemed he hadn't heard her approach, and she was able to admire the tight lines of his arse, and the way he moved as he worked.

The knife in his hand looked sharp and dangerous. Shane thought it might not be a good idea to get too close without letting him know she was there. She rapped on the door.

Ross spun around with the knife still held at a dangerous angle between his fingers. When he took in her attire, he looked at her with a puzzled expression. "You've not showered." It wasn't a question.

Was it hurt she saw in his eyes? "I'm about to, but well…" Shane hesitated, unsure how to voice her fears. *Bite the bullet, woman. Just go for it.* "Ah hell, I need to know. Are you involved with anyone at all?" The words tumbled out and she cursed the way she spoke. "Look, I know that sounds presumptuous and stuff, and I can't imagine you are but... Well I've been burned once, oh, not physically, though I'm sure there's burns and burns and oh, shit, I'm babbling. No, hell and, oh fuck, you hate swearing and I've bloody done it again. No not burns, heat and stuff and fuck it, Shane, shut your mouth." She took a deep breath and folded her arms across her middle. "Anyway, I had to ask."

Ross put the knife down and leaned back on the edge of the work surface, his hands braced on the marble top. "Why? You said you're not interested, so why should it bother you?" His voice was level and almost uninterested. He sounded as if he was asking her the time or something equally as mundane.

It was deserved, but the urge to know hadn't diminished. Maybe now she needed to open up a little more?

"Look, Ross, once I've spoken to Jess, I'll explain. But until then, I can't. But, I need to know."

"Why? It's an insult." He turned his back on her and thumped the knife down into a poor, unsuspecting vegetable. Bits of carrot skittered over the work surface and onto the floor. "Go take a shower, Shane." The name sounded like an insult as well. "I'll have some food ready when you get back. You don't owe me any explanations, nor I you."

"Dammit, don't you turn your back on me, Ross Mackie. I can't tell you 'til I've spoken to Jess, okay. It's not all my story to tell." She poked him in the back. "Stop acting as if you've spat your dummy out, man up, pull up your big boy boxers and listen to me. You say you're a Dom, so bloody act like one."

His back stiffened.

"And damn well look at me when I shout at you."

His shoulders moved. Shane poked him again. "Or fuck you, I'm out of here."

That made him turn. The knife clattered into the sink as he threw it away from them.

"Shane, you questioned my integrity, both as a man and a Dom. It not only hurts, it's offensive. Do you really think I'd be so crass as to indicate I want to play with you, when I already have a sub or a partner?"

"Some people do." Try as she might, she couldn't keep her voice level.

"Some do, I don't. If I did, I would have told you that right back at the beginning of our conversations." He kissed her nose. It tickled and Shane wrinkled it. Ross laughed. "I can see you're a bratty sub, kitten. I like that. Okay, before you call me out again, let's try this. Hypothetically if you *are* a sub, you *would* be a bratty one. How's that?"

Shane smiled. He said it so patiently, but with a glint in his eye that showed her exactly what he thought she was. He was correct, but she had no intention of telling him. Not until… She dragged her mind away from dark thoughts. "Better. And I agree. Hypothetically if I *was* a sub, I so would be."

"It could make life interesting then. *If* you're a sub. Go have your shower, Shane." This time her name sounded normal, not an epithet. "Get warm, and then we can move on."

She nodded and grinned. Everything seemed brighter, and Shane realized she hadn't felt so full of hope and enthusiasm for ages. She almost skipped back to the bedroom, where she did a shimmy to help her clammy denims over her hips then grimaced as the cold damp material chafed her skin. Was there anything worse?

Well, yes, there was a lot, but at that moment, it came very high up the list. Shane got rid of the offending garment just as there was a knock on the bedroom door. She looked around her for something to cover her bottom half. Hot pink socks and a scarlet thong wasn't exactly sartorially elegant, especially with a fuzzy blue jumper covering her top. She hadn't thought about color co-ordination when she'd dressed, more about warmth.

"Shane, I've clothes here for you."

"Um, er, okay, half a sec." She did the best thing she could think of and slid under the duvet. Okay, I'm decent."

The door opened and Ross came in with a large stuffed bag. "Pity. Or are you in there waiting for me?" His eyes twinkled and Shane guessed he was now trying to reassure her all was okay in their world.

"In your dreams," she said inelegantly.

"Oh yeah, you've got that right." He dumped the bag on top of a chair. "Should be something that'll work in here." Ross picked up her jeans and walked back to the door "Shove the rest of your wet clothes outside and I'll put them in the dryer."

Shane stared at the door as it closed behind him and let her breath out in one long sigh. Her simple idea of meet Jess, chat and move on, was suddenly a whole lot more complicated. She got out of the bed, smoothed the duvet and shoved the rest of her clothes outside the door as Ross had directed. Then she made her way into the bathroom to stand under the hot shower until her skin tingled. Eventually she forced herself out from under the gentle, soothing spray and made her way back to the bedroom with a towel tightly twisted around her. Silly, because of course

Ross wouldn't be there, however that little bit of protection mattered.

The bag on the chair had fallen over and some of the contents had spilled onto the carpet. Something bright caught her eye and Shane walked across the room and stared at the scarlet silk that shimmered in the lamp light. That wasn't sweats or joggers. She picked the material up between her thumb and forefinger. It was revealed as a very sexy, slinky, soft slip of a dress, with tiny thin straps and a pretty scalloped hem. A scrap of paper was pinned to it.

Not joggers but much more you, I think. I dare you.

Shane stared at the dress and dropped it as if it was hot. Then she picked it up again and held it next to her cheek. Nice, but *so* not her.

By the time she returned to the lounge, Ross was once more sat on the sofa, legs stretched out in front of him with his ankles crossed and his arms behind his head. His shirt and jeans stretched tightly over his body gave Shane the perfect idea of how fit and well-honed he was. She risked a quick look toward his cock and bit back a groan. The outline there was one big, juice-inducing bulge. She swallowed as she salivated at the thought of that anywhere near her.

Oh, my yes please.

Ross looked up at her and smiled. "Feel better?"

*Well, I do and I don't. S*he didn't think she'd say that though. "Yes, thank you. I hope you don't mind me in the dressing gown? Those joggers slid off me as soon as I moved." She didn't mention the dress.

"Whatever you feel happiest in is fine by me."

He didn't mention the dress either. Had she hoped he would?

Raven McAllan

"Coffee on its way." Ross stood up. "I've rustled up soup. Do you want it now?"

Her tummy had so many butterflies in it, she felt sick and she had to clench her fists to stop her hands shaking. She didn't envisage her managing to drink soup without spilling it down her cleavage, and maybe a dash to the loo. "Later, I think."

"No worries. I'll grab coffee and biccies instead for now then. Oh, by the way, I've just had a phone call from Jess. She and David are stuck in town. They've had to take a hotel room. There was a really disgusted note in her voice. I think they'd earmarked one of the dungeons for themselves tonight, seeing as the club is closed. One of the perks of being co-owner." He disappeared into the kitchen, and the clinks and chinks of crockery being moved drifted toward her.

It seemed Jess had gotten over her bad experience then. However, until she heard the lady tell her so, Shane wouldn't settle, or decide what she might do. Stupid and irrational, she knew, but it niggled. And niggles weren't something Shane ever chose to ignore these days, not since she had ignored her itch between the shoulder blades niggle over Pete. What a mistake that had been.

"Hmm, I guess." Shane nibbled her lip as she sat on the sofa and pulled the dressing gown around her. How much could she say? She had to give some sort of explanation, but it was so difficult.

"Here you go." Ross had re-entered without Shane noticing, and put her coffee and a ceramic biscuit tin shaped like a dick or vibrator on the table next to her. Shane looked at him and sniggered. It was so out of place in such a masculine room. "And this is yours?"

"Sadly yes. It was a housewarming present from Jess and Kath, who said I was getting staid."

Staid wasn't a word she would apply to him. "They have, ah, unusual tastes."

"Weird sense of humor, more like. Bratty subs both of them. Even having her babies hasn't slowed Kath down. Luckily, both David and Jeff have their measures." His fondness for the two couples was evident in the way he spoke about them

Will he ever talk about me in that tone? Oh, God, I hope so. I want my chance now. Surely I deserve that?

"Anyway," Ross continued. "The biscuits aren't cock shaped." He paused and winked. "I've eaten those. These are nipples."

Shane stopped just as she was about to dip into the tin. "You prefer nipples to cocks then?"

Ross roared with laughter. "Every time, kitten, every bloody time."

"You swore," Shane said. "You won't let me." She pulled out a biscuit. A long oblong, ordinary shortbread. You lied as well. This isn't a nipple."

"I must have eaten all the nipples then." Ross didn't sound at all repentant. "I apologize for my language. Maybe I need pussies next?"

Pussy singular if I have any say in the matter. For one awful moment, Shane thought she'd spoken aloud. It was hard not to exhale heavily when she realized she hadn't.

"Well, whatever turns you on."

"You, it seems." Ross looked down at the outline of his cock straining the denim of his jeans. "I hope this denim is a strong as the makers boast, or I'm in trouble. You'd never believe it was an accident."

"I would so. I'm not that stupid," Shane said, stung at his assumption she was so shallow. "No one would rip two-hundred dollar jeans on purpose. Well, not with their cock, think of the grazes you'd get."

He winked.

"You sod, you're taking the p..." She stopped mid-sentence. She wanted to try to not swear. "You're taking the mickey."

"Just a bit, kitten. Sorry." However, he didn't look the least bit sorry.

Ross leaned over her and selected a biscuit. "However, I stand by the fact these jeans are now bloody uncomfortable." As he straightened up, his elbow hooked in the neckline of her dressing gown, and made it gape. A slither of red showed.

She tugged it back to where it was, but she should have known Ross would have noticed and put two and two together. Doms were trained to be aware of every nuance and action, and Ross wasn't anywhere near unobservant.

"Kitten, what have we here?" He ran his finger across her neck and along the edge of the V. His knuckles grazed her soft skin then rubbed the material. It tightened over her breasts and her sensitive nipples peaked against the silk. That friction set up a corresponding tingle in her pussy and clit. Damned if she wouldn't be dampening the stuff if she wasn't careful. And wet red showed up so clearly.

"Ah..." Shane bet her face was the color of the material she'd intended to keep hidden until she was ready to reveal it.

"Ah'?" Ross asked her. "As in ah-tishoo? Ah-titchoke? Or, ah, well it's like this?"

"The latter. The joggers really did fall off me."

Ross nodded, that was why he'd left that particular set for her to use. He chose not to mention a short, to the point email he'd had from her brothers. Something along the lines of mess her up you're dead, help her and you're not. He'd thought the red dress was worth a try, and he'd bet she was stunning in it.

"So why the dressing gown? Don't you like the dress?" There was no point in skirting the issue.

"I love it, but there's not much of it, and well, it's one thing putting it on and pretending it's my nightie—another prancing around in it and B all else." She rolled her eyes. "I'm not much of an exhibitionist. Never was."

You will be with me. Ross loved being able to show how fantastic his sub was. One of his preferred methods of making a sub fly was either by Shibari and rigging, or with a crop or flogger, and showing how she did so to whoever was around in the club. If Shane only wanted to play in private, he'd go for it, but a big chunk of who he was would be missing.

Hold on, she's not even admitted she's a sub, let alone said she'd sub for you or what her preferences were. It was all hypothetical, remember. All he recollected she'd admitted to was the statement she didn't do pain, which was a pity. However, hopefully he could show her there was pain, and there was *pleasure* in pain. If she let him.

"We'll see," Ross said, noncommittally. "Mind you, it's warm in here, and there's only me to see you." He tugged at the messy knot in the gown's sash. "So there's no need to cover up."

To his delight she let him undo the sash, and draw the sides of the robe apart. The red silk hugged her breasts like a lover and skimmed across her belly, emphasizing her feminine curves and the shape of her pussy, to end mid-thigh. Ross didn't try to hide himself moving his cock away from the zip teeth of his jeans. "Stand up and let me look, kitten, please." He couched it so they had a starting point to go on from afterwards.

Shane touched her nose before she slowly stood up, without letting go of the sleeves of the dressing gown.

"Drop it, kitten." He did inject a note of command then, and Shane blinked before she unclenched her fingers from the cuffs of the material and let it fall to the seat of the settee.

She lowered her eyes and crossed her arms over her boobs. "I feel naked. And I'm not doing anything until I've spoken to Jess."

Does she think that if she says that often enough we'll both believe it?

"Uncross your arms. You look beautiful, and nowhere near naked, kitten. That can come later."

Shane shook her head and didn't move her arms. "I don't do naked, I told you. This is almost as bad. It's practically see-through. You can make out all of me through it."

Ross took hold of her arms and placed them by her sides. "Rubbish, though I see a hint of hair that needs removing."

"Ross." Shane squeaked the word and blushed the color of her dress. Her arms moved.

"Keep them there."

"R...o...ss. Sir." She might sound embarrassed, but her nipples were still hard against the material and she pressed her thighs together.

"I like my pussy naked," he said. "No clothes, no pussy hair. You'll do it one day. Or I can do it for you."

She shook her head. "Oh, blimey, Ross, don't get your hopes up. Ah, how embarrassing, talking about my muff. Sheesh. Seriously, I might not get any further than this. This is a biggie for me. It's been long skirts and oversized baggy jumpers these last few years. I will tell you why, soon, hopefully."

Her toes scrunched up in the deep pile of the carpet until the shiny pink nail varnish he'd noticed couldn't be seen anymore. "But not yet."

He understood he'd get no more information. Therefore he'd move them forward in a different way.

"All right. Are you ready for a look around? Bearing in mind there's only us here and no one else will see you."

He held his breath.

Very slowly, she nodded. "Yes, Sir."

Chapter Five

Oh, Lord, what have I committed myself to? Nothing except to look around. I had to call him Sir. It would be disrespectful not to, especially as he's showing me the club. But what if he thinks it means I'll sub? Because I don't know and, oh, fuck, I want to go home.

"Kitten, I can see your thoughts rushing through you like a whirlwind. Slow down. We're walking through a closed club — no more, no less. Then we'll come back up here for dinner, and for the rest of the evening, I'll defer to you and your desire."

"No Domming?" She couldn't believe he'd agree to that. He showed he was a Dom in everything he said and did. It was an integral part of him, whether he knew it or not.

"No Domming," he agreed, to Shane's surprise. "Unless you say, Ross, please be a Dom to me. Okay?"

"More likelihood of a snowball surviving in hell than that." As he'd been so accommodating, Shane decided she could meet him half way. "But I will call you Sir until we get back here."

"That's a good enough start for me." Ross smiled and tilted his head downwards until he could kiss the nape of her neck. His fresh, minty breath swirled around her and filled her senses. The nip and suck was so slight she wondered if she'd dreamt it. Then he lifted his lips. "One day, kitten, I'll bite you and leave my mark."

"Not where it shows you won't," Shane said in as firm a tone as she could manage. Damned if the thought didn't make her wet and her clit throb. "I hate hickeys."

"You won't when I give one to you. That first light nip, the deep pull as I suck, the final bite and the throbbing. Plus the knowledge I've marked you as mine as surely as if I've whipped your arse." He lifted his head and winked. "Barefoot and bare arsed. Perfect."

Damned if that wink doesn't make me wet and go all gooey, every time.

"Hypothetically speaking, of course."

"Oh, of course," Shane said. She was beginning to hate that word — *hypothetically.*

"If we ever get together to play, I warn you it will be full on, Dom and sub — and more."

There's more? Shane could no more stop the red, rosy hue suffusing her than she could have swam with a crocodile.

He laughed. "Come on. Let's go."

Ross took her arm and cuddled her into his side as he urged her out of the room and away from the direction of the lift. His other hand rested firmly on her buttocks, and she had an idea his pinkie teased the entrance to her arse. Surely he wouldn't? Not here and now? He made no mention of how he held her as they moved together, and Shane decided to just enjoy the feeling of unity.

The warmth of his body was more than welcome. Embraced as she was, she felt safe and cherished and it hit her that the intensity of her emotions was unexpected. Why did the simple act of being cuddled as she walked matter so much? Shane hadn't got a clue, but she wasn't going to dismiss her feelings out of hand. They pleased her.

"I thought we were going to the club?"

"We are, but not by the lift. That takes us to the wrong place. Hold on a sec." It was another fingerprint recognition pad. "We had these put in a while back when someone broke in. That was a doozy of a time. It ended okay, and one of our Doms and his sub are together because of it, but it was worrying. Still is, in one way, because not all the mystery was solved."

"You didn't catch the intruder?" Shane was interested. She loved a mystery—as long as it didn't involve her. She'd had enough problems in her past to not want any more. "Or they wouldn't spill the beans?"

"Nah, well, not quite. We caught an intruder, who was a goody, and missed catching the white van man—or woman—who was a baddy. No beans were hurt in the process."

Shane snorted. His sense of humor was as wacky as hers. "That's as clear as mud," she said as they entered yet another corridor and Ross swiped yet another pad.

"Hold on." Something he'd said rang a bell and she stopped dead and dragged Ross to a standstill. "White van?"

"Yeah, ba...er, bandits. Why?"

"I nearly got run off the road by a white van on my way here. Say around ten minutes before I turned into your drive. On the windy, crappy apology for a lane I used to get here from the main road. Why don't they just call it unsealed and be done with it. All this uneven surface rubbish is so misleading."

"Not if you live here," Ross said. "It is uneven."

"Hmm, if you say so. It was covered with snow, so I couldn't tell."

"The van?" Ross prompted her.

"The van. It came out of it like a bat out of hell, swerved in the slushy snow and drove off like crazy. Mind you, I didn't see if it was a man or a woman driving. To be honest, I was more concerned with staying on the road and not getting close up and personal with the ditch or later on, your gatepost."

"Are you okay?" Ross took her chin in his hand and tilted her head so she looked him in the eyes.

Shane nodded. "Yeah, I just used all those words you hate."

"Thank God. Nevertheless, we'll still tell our local cops when we get the chance. No point in rushing to do it now, any traces will be well obliterated. I guess there's no use asking if you saw the number plate or if it had anything written on the side?"

"Nope, not at all. Though…" Shane concentrated. "I can't swear to it, but I think one of the headlights was out. I was more concerned with saving my arse. Not that that's a lot of help, eh? Easily replaced." She shrugged. "The headlight, not my arse. That is irreplaceable."

"Sure is." Ross patted her rear and pinched it. "Perfect."

"Damn it though, I *am* sorry I'm no more use. Why did someone want to break in?"

"Hey, no worries to the rest, you did more than most people could, I reckon. The break in was sort of official. No don't ask. I can't tell you, it's all police confidentiality and such like. I'll ring Ailsa and tell her what you told me. She'll be interested to hear it."

"Ailsa?" The surge of white hot jealousy annoyed Shane. Just because he said the name with such affection didn't mean anything other than…well, affection. Did it?

"A friend in the force, who is the partner of another friend." The way he couched his words was as big a giveaway as if he'd said friends in the lifestyle. Shane didn't comment. After all, she knew about privacy and discretion.

"However," Ross said. "The white van we're still worried about. There's been stuff moved around the estate, cottages used for something or other and lots of digging."

"Dead bodies? Buried treasure?"

"Ropes and barbed wire. Puzzling."

Shane laughed. "Well the barbed wire is not to my taste at all, and I'm not keen on ropes, but each to their own. Why bury it though? Don't you have lockers?"

Ross pinched her chin. "Trust you to say what I reckon some of the local police thought."

"Only some? You have kinky police?"

"Well, why not. Kink doesn't have an agenda of who is and who isn't."

This Ailsa maybe?

Shane would love to know who was and who wasn't, but it wasn't something you ever asked. She accepted she was just nosy. She needed to curtail that propensity. Look where it had gotten her with Pete.

"Okay, this is our control room." Ross ushered her into a rectangular room, with a bank of angled windows on one side plus a row of security screens and telephones on another. "We can oversee everything from here. Even if someone chooses a private room, they sign up to security cameras from here. Security—and the knowledge you're safe from being sued or arrested—is paramount."

"One reason for scening here and not at home?" To Shane's annoyance, her voice wavered.

Ross gave her a sharp look. "In some cases, yes. Especially in a new relationship. Although a lot of our members have been together for a long time, they still enjoy scening here. And socializing as well. It's not all whips and wax."

He switched on one of the screens. "See how we can look without being intrusive? It's all safety first." The screen lit up with a view of what looked like the lounge area.

"What if the Dom ignores his sub's safe word?" Shane had to ask.

Ross gave her another of those looks that seemed to sear into her soul. "He'll never Dom again anywhere we know of. Safe words are sacrosanct."

"But how would you always know?" Shane persisted. "They're down there and you're up here. You can't always see the signs, can you?" A horrid familiar sick feeling crept over her, and she swallowed the bile that threatened to appear. She'd thought she was past it. How wrong could you be?

"Come hell or high water, kitten, I'm going to get to the bottom of what puts that look into your eyes. Hold on." He flicked another switch. The screen changed from the lounge with its plush seats, to show a room with a St, Andrew's cross and a spanking bench, plus a bed a bit like a masseur's chair and several cupboards. Hanging from the ceiling were hooks and

D rings and a vertical metal bar. Shane did her best not to ogle or let her instant arousal show. The more she saw and learned, the more Poisonous Pete the Plonker retreated. Now, once she saw Jess, the past would hopefully be well dead and buried.

"Well?" Ross asked her. "You haven't run away screaming yet."

"No, not yet," Shane agreed. "But..."

"Stay here and watch the monitor. I won't be long." He pushed a chair under her bum, dropped a swift kiss on the top of her head and left the room at a jog.

Unable to settle, Shane stood up and wandered around looking at the consoles and at a series of photos on the walls. Several depicted a couple, who were obviously well into a scene. She peered closely and stared at the expression on the woman's face. It was serene, calm and she seemed totally at ease and happy with her position, rigged in an intricate harness of knots and ties, suspended several feet above the ground. Even her hair was tied. It was something Shane had often wondered about, but never experienced. After Pete, she hadn't thought she'd ever want to. The Dom who stood beside the lady exuded confidence and total command, and he bent his head and, Shane surmised, asked the sub a question.

Something about the way he stood rang a bell. She moved her attention from the woman to the Dom. As she thought, it was Ross. The jealousy that filled her came as a surprise.

I want him to do that to me. She thought about it as she made her way back to the original screen Ross had asked her to stop by and sat down again. The screen showed the door opening and closing, then Ross appeared in the room. He turned and looked up toward where the camera must be sited.

"Hello, kitten. I'm hoping you can hear me. If you can, press the switch in the console, marked 'speak' and say so."

Shane looked along the row of switches, found the one she wanted and pressed it. "I can hear you."

"So if I had a poor innocent little subbie strapped down on here"—he stroked the soft top of the spanking bench—"or rigged up and swinging." He set one of the metal rings moving. "And ignored her shouting, or"—he lowered his voice—"whispering red or whatever, would it be ignored? Bearing in mind the control room is monitored all the time by two people, as well as a dungeon master in each room. We take safe, sane and consensual very seriously, kitten, as do all sensible clubs and Doms. Heard enough?"

"Yes, Sir, and thank you. I feel silly now."

"Kitten." His voice was harsh, and Shane flinched. Had she annoyed him so much?

"Never ever feel silly for being safety conscious. It's not thinking ahead and paying attention to your safety that's silly. Stay there. I'll be back in a minute."

He left the dungeon and sure enough, within a minute the control room door opened and Ross walked in.

"Ready for a wander now?"

It didn't occur to her that she was about to do something she never ever thought she'd do again. Shane stood up, walked toward Ross and dropped to her knees. Very deliberately she put her hands behind her back and bent her head to look at the floor by his bare feet. She remembered from years before that he hated shoes and kicked them off at every opportunity.

"Yes, please, Sir."

He tugged her hair so she looked up at him. "That, kitten, is a lovely sight. I hope I'll see more of it, but for now, welcome to my world."

Chapter Six

As he looked down at Shane, something indefinable filled Ross's mind. It wasn't just seeing a woman he wanted on her knees as a sub, but also the total trust in her expression that gladdened him. Even as a child, her solemn expression and need to know everything had fascinated him. For a brief second, the difference in their ages worried him. Was twelve years too much? In reality, why should it be? As long as he could get the image of baby snatching and dirty old men out of his mind... She was well over the age of consent now, and until he'd seen her again he hadn't thought of her as anything except Troy and Jase's younger, pesky, nosy sister.

Now though, everything had changed. The only connection with Jase and Troy was his knowledge that if he messed her up, they'd string him up by the balls. He might like Shibari and love rigging, but having it happen to him around those valuable nuts didn't bear thinking about. It was all he could do not to cup his palm over that area of his body.

"Do you mean that, kitten? You're happy to sub to me? Because if you do, we start now." He was damned sure that she'd probably cry red, now or after she saw what he liked.

"Ross, please be a Dom to me."

She'd remembered his promise. Once again she surprised him. Her eyes widened and she leaned into him, seemingly unheeding of the sting it must give her scalp.

"I'm happy, Sir, because I trust you to listen to me. Even though I'd promised myself nothing until I speak to Jess."

There was definitely an undercurrent. *All tied in with her need to speak to Jess? No matter, I'll be patient.* He hoped. Although he had infinite patience in a scene and drew out the best in every one he played with, outside that sphere, Ross knew he wasn't renowned for his patience.

"I will never ignore you or give you a reason to doubt me, kitten. That's a promise. So, up you get." He tugged on her hair, and Shane stood up straight in front of him. She blinked, swallowed and looked down at the floor once more.

"Kitten, there's only us here, no need to do that. Although when we scene in the club with others around, I'd expect it."

She paled. "Red."

"Red? Red what?" He would make her spell it out, even if it ended there and then.

"Nothing in public. Hard limit there. I am not showing my wobbly bits or my vulnerability to any old passerby with a hint of kink in them. If, and I'm stressing the if, we do anything beyond tonight, I'm for you to see and you only."

Ross wondered if she truly thought that. Her skin was once more glowing and her ashen hue had disappeared. If she did, then there would need to be a lot of hard thinking done by both of them.

"If you're for me to see, then strip." He hadn't known that he was going to say that until the words were spoken.

"Strip?" She squeaked the words. "As in, take this apology for a dress off? It's see-through, so why take it off?"

"Why keep it on? If it's see-through, then there's no point in wearing it. It's not cold in here. And we won't be doing anything other than looking around, kitten. Here... Arms up." He took hold of the hem of her dress and began to lift it over her body.

"We won't?" Shane lifted her arms obediently and stood still until he removed the dress.

"No, we won't."

She began to move her arms over her boobs and pussy.

"Kitten."

She stopped instantly and let them drop to her sides.

"If we were to play tonight," Ross said as he urged her forward with a none too soft tap to her arse — damned if he didn't ache to do more than a tap, "then I'd tie your arms behind you. Your body is beautiful, and once we get rid of your pussy hair, it'll be even more so." He didn't give her a chance to argue or protest as he pushed her out of the control room and along the corridor to the nearest stairs.

"Of course we could take the lift, but I'd rather see you sway as you go down the stairs."

She sniggered. "Sway is an understatement. You do know my boobs will ache without any upholstery?"

"You should have chosen the corset then. Your choice, your suffering. Accept it or red."

Shane descended five or six stairs and turned round to look at him. "You're a sadist."

"Of course, and that's sadist, Sir, to you. Go through the door at the bottom and turn left. You'll come to the lounge."

"Yes, sadist, Sir."

Damned if he didn't want to laugh. Scared stiff, aroused — her pert nipples and the damp hair on her pussy showed that — she still gave him backchat. Good for her. His Shane was one spunky sub.

My Shane? He thought about it. He damned well hoped so. Ross waited with scarcely concealed impatience as Shane nodded, turned around and continued down the stairs. Next time, he vowed, he'd have her walk up the stairs in front of him, then back down again, just so he got a perfect view of her in all her naked glory. Even thinking about it made his cock twitch.

Shane disappeared from view and Ross took the remaining stairs two at a time and caught up with her as she entered the lounge and did a slow circle to take everything in. He tried to see it through her eyes. Gray leather settees — easy to wipe down and sanitize — rings on the floor next to some of them, the sort you'd tie a dog to, lots of large soft cushions and plenty of low tables. Apart from the hooks, it was just what you'd see in any lounge.

"Normal," Shane said, surprise in her voice. "It could be anywhere. Posh hotel, squash club, anywhere."

"What did you expect? This is as vanilla as anywhere outside. Nothing happens in here, except chatting, eating and if you're not playing, a drink.

Except the subs may be half naked, and on a leash. Each to their own. Leashes are not my thing."

Shane wandered from the bar to the long, squashy settees, looked at the ring hooks in the floor and shuddered. "Thank goodness for some small mercies then. Now, I guess this is the time to ask you that all important question. Sir, what *is* your thing?"

He'd wondered when she was going to broach that subject.

Chapter Seven

The long heard and never understood phrase, 'a pregnant silence' suddenly became clear to Shane. Ross studied her as if he'd never seen her before and rolled his shoulders as if to de-knot the muscles. Eventually he beckoned to her.

"Follow me." He turned on his bare heel without waiting to see if she obeyed him or not.

Shane walked after him. Her bare feet slapped on the floor, just as Ross' had and she was glad the surface looked spotless. Unfortunately she could see her reflection in the polished surface and watch her boobs and arse jiggle as she walked. Sleek and svelte she wasn't. However, as it didn't seem to bother Ross—just the opposite—why should she worry? She was what she was, and diet didn't enter her vocabulary. She ate sensibly and that was it.

Ross walked to the far end of a softly lit corridor and waited until she reached him. "Up ourselves or what, but through this door are our private rooms—rooms that are strictly used by a selected few people only, and ones we never share. I was lucky enough to be given one."

"Is that normal, Sir?"

His smile gave Shane a soft, tingly sensation, and made her wetter to the extent she knew damn well if he glanced down it'd be easily visible on her thighs. If one look did that, heaven help her if they ever did play. She'd need wringing out.

"Define normal."

He had a point.

"Do many clubs do that? Give rooms to one person only?"

Ross shrugged. "I've no idea. This is all down to the lady you want to meet, and her buddy. Jess and Kath decided we need our own dungeons, because sometimes being the boss or whatever means no peace for the wicked. You'd come to play and be stopped to give advice or have people wanting to watch, that you'd not even get started before it was time to stop. Because none of us only want to be able to play on the nights the club is closed, unless we want to scene in public, we created this area. There's another stair from the control room corridor as well, so we have the option to bypass the club. My room has been little used lately. My last sub and I parted ways—amicably, I may add—a few months ago, before we really got into a Dom/sub relationship. We found we worked better as friends. She's pretty busy with her job, so we don't see that much of her. Before you ask, if I have needed a sub for a demo, Connie has obliged, but that's it. Who knows, now you might do it for me."

"I'll be back in Freo."

Not if I have my way, you won't. "Maybe. Maybe not. So, kitten, would you like to see my dungeon? Then we'll do the public ones." Why had he decided to do what most people would say was the suicidal way round? Because he wanted her to know him and his ways first and foremost. Then if it was an 'oh, no, not in a million years', he'd give her the tamer view, before showing her to her bedroom.

"You know, I think I would." She sounded surprised, as if she hadn't known she was going to say that. "Sir."

Ross tapped her on the nose. "Remembered just in time, eh, kitten?"

"Yup, it's alien to me. The only Sir I remember is the stupid sodding classics teacher at uni, and why I had to take a module in classics, God only knows. I was studying politics. Anyway, Sir, lead on."

Amused by her ramblings, her out and out challenge of everything they did plus her unexpected acceptance of what they were doing, Ross mentally laughed and swiped his thumb over the pad by the door handle.

The click as the lock disengaged was loud in the quiet corridor, and Shane jumped. "Is this where you do the 'come into my parlor, said the spider to the fly' bit?"

"Maybe my room is your room?" Ross said as he stood back to let her precede him into his dungeon. "Or make yourself at home."

"Ha, I don't think comfortable is what you have in mind in here — not in the conventional sense anyway." She walked passed Ross and stopped dead, before she turned around, arms spread wide. The pose exposed every inch and cranny of her, and Ross swallowed as his body tightened as he admired all of her.

Shane giggled and curtseyed. Her self-consciousness about her nakedness seemed to be a thing of the past. "Sh…sugarooney."

He hadn't heard that expression of astonishment for years, but he could well echo it.

Shane pointed toward the narrow bed with its firm mattress and carved wooden fittings situated at the rear of the room. "Nice one. But I bet it's not for sleeping on."

"You can if you want. I prefer to use it for orgasm denial."

"Oh, blimey. I don't have enough to be denied those I do get." She put her hand over her mouth. "Sheesh, verbal diarrhea or what? Scratch that. Delete it from your mind, please, Sir."

"Not a chance, kitten. Are you telling me you don't do self help? That you do your own self-denial?"

"I'm saying nothing." She mimed zipping her lips. "Not on that subject anyway."

"You think?" He had to prod her. She rose so beautifully to his teasing.

"I know. Anyway, changing the subject somewhat, can I touch things?"

He inclined his head. "If you ask nicely and tell me why, kitten."

Shane nodded and looked up above her head where a large metal ring and bar hung attached to a pulley system on the wall.

"Shibari? I've never seen stuff in reality."

"Yes. Want to try?"

She shook her head and once more created a cape with her hair. Ross muttered to himself. He'd meant to tie it up earlier, just to show her every facet of how they would play—if they ever did. His usually level mood was mercurial, to say the least. It seesawed between positive and negative thoughts with regards to whether they'd play or not, that it was a wonder he wasn't giddy. Should he ask why? Ross decided to leave his questions until she'd asked all of hers. For one moment he wondered if it wise. From what he'd seen, she could ask questions until the cows came home, and probably would if she had an inkling it would save her from answering any herself.

"Can I look in the cupboard?"

"Help yourself, kitten. But remember, curiosity killed the cat."

She snorted. "And maimed the kitten?"

"Let's hope not. You're welcome to look anywhere. I have no secrets from you."

The words, 'not like you have from me', hung in the air over them, like a black cloud of doubt. Once again Ross had the gut churning sensation of losing control, and it didn't sit well on him. He was a Dom, for heaven's sake, and should be in a position to take care of his sub, and sort out her worries and fears. The niggling voice telling him she wasn't his sub, he ignored. She would be. She had to be.

"Oh, hell...p, Sir, I hope I won't soon with you." Shane unlatched the floor to ceiling cupboard door and looked at the contents. "You like your floggers then?" She put her head into the cupboard and her voice became muffled. "There's enough stuff in here to open a saddlery or an ironmonger. Why do you need it all?"

"My crops, whips, blindfolds and shackles?" Ross asked. "To say nothing of my Shibari ropes? I like to be well prepared. I'm a simple soul, with simple tastes."

"Yeah, and the moon is made of cream cheese, Sir." Shane closed the door and leaned on the varnished wood surface, her legs close together. "So, Sir, what would you say you're a master in?"

Ross studied her flushed face and noticed how her breasts heaved as she breathed erratically. Her skin was covered in a soft bloom, which he was sure was due to her arousal, and he'd bet she stood as she did to hide the evidence that confirmed it.

"Rigging and flogging. Spanking and Shibari. Oh, and a little bit of orgasm denial." He studied her face as her mouth opened in a silent gasp. "Or forced orgasm. It depends on my mood."

"A bit of a sadist, Sir?"

"Not a bit, kitten." He waited until her eyes widened and she shut her mouth and blinked. "Totally." It was an exaggeration, but Ross had decided to go to the extremes of his tastes and see if it fazed her. "There's something so beautiful and satisfying in knowing I've pushed my sub way past what she thought she'd accept and more, without her even thinking of safe-wording out. Pain is pleasure. Believe me."

"You reckon? There's pain and there's pain, Sir. I don't do pain—or bondage." Shane whispered something and Ross strained to hear what she said. It sounded like, 'not any more'.

"You will, kitten. Once you decide to trust me to know what you want and how to give it to you."

"Ah, well, who knows? However, as an observer, your dungeon is very you," Shane said somewhat cryptically. "Sir, can we go back to hypothetically again?"

Shane pushed herself up off the door and stood straight in front of him, with her hands neatly tucked behind her back. She was, Ross decided, such a mass of contradictions. One moment scared, uncertain, questioning every last thing and looking as if she'd love to whip the subbie blanket off the back of the chair and cover herself, the next unconscious of her surroundings and state of dress, and so much a sub, it was beautiful to see. The sooner she spoke to Jess and got whatever it was sorted out, the better.

"When we get out of here, why not?" If it was the way to get answers, Ross was all for hypothetical. "Have you seen enough, kitten?" He moved toward her and held his hand out. She took it and let him cuddle her in. Her hair tickled his arms, and her breath caressed his skin like a lover. Her hands at the base of his spine were warm, and gave him hope.

"Because standing in here with you is testing my patience to the limit," Ross went on. "This is my dungeon, where I know I can make you enjoy things you've probably never dreamed of. Show you what a perfect sub you are and how good we would be together." Never again was he going to give her a chance to doubt his intentions. It would be will and when, not maybe or if. "Apart from that, I'm so fucking hard, I'm the one in pain. I can't make up my mind in what order I'd like to do first. Fuck you or make you fly."

Chapter Eight

Well that was telling her his intentions with a vengeance. Shane put her arms around Ross, and decided naked or not, she liked being close to him. Of course it would be easier in clothes—her wet legs and damp pussy hair wouldn't be so obvious then. Every word he'd said curled around her like a warm blanket and increased her arousal. It was getting harder and harder not to just give in and sub liked she wanted to.

It was something she'd never thought could or would happen, and here she was denying herself the chance to experience everything her dreams were made of. One of the reasons she'd been attracted to Pete the Plonker was she'd thought he reminded her of Ross. Now of course she wondered how she'd deluded herself so easily. They were chalk and cheese.

Shane almost bit her lip but stopped herself just in time. Damn it, why couldn't Jess have been around? More to the point, why was it so damned important she made certain Jess had moved on and her brothers hadn't scared or scarred her in any way, before she, Shane, moved on herself?

"Sir, can you tell me honestly without sharing stuff you shouldn't, how Jess is?" *Shit, I sound needy and weedy and pathetic. And I can't even say pull up my big girl panties, I'm not wearing any.* "It's really important."

"Hypothetically?"

"No, really. Hypothetical is if I did say I'd sub, could we go slowly?"

The look he gave her could shrivel leaves faster than the sun back home.

"If you have to ask that, there's no point in continuing."

Shane lost her temper. "Fuck you, Mr. up-his-own-arse-so-far-he's-blind Mackie." She screamed the words, pushed his arms off her, stalked stiff legged to the bed and thumped the mattress. It was that or him and at least the mattress wouldn't hit back. As her hand met the surface, she wasn't so sure. There wasn't a lot of give in it, and the jolt went right up her arm. She bit back even more swear words.

"I want to say yes. I want to roll over onto my back and shout, take me I'm yours, but I can't, not yet. I want to keep saying, Ross, please be a Dom to me until you believe me and do it. But, how the hell can I have my happiness when I don't know if Jess has hers? And if she hasn't, is it all my fault for not speaking out? I need to know first. I need to know."

She sat down heavily on the bed and cradled her wrist. It still throbbed where she'd thumped it.

"Shit, that bloody hurts."

"That's five so far," Ross said in a level tone. "Want to make it a nice round half dozen?"

"Eh?" *What on earth is he going on about?* "You've lost me here."

"Cuss words. Five spanks per word. I'll remember."

Even in her agitated state, that pronouncement made her wetter and more turned on than she'd have thought possible. It was almost worth adding something more to his list. Almost.

"Look," Shane said desperately. "Is she okay? Even if you can't tell me any more than that, is Jess...well, I dunno, normal?"

Ross burst out laughing and Shane clenched her fists. *Infuriating, awkward, pain in the...*

"No, kitten, don't hit me. You'll regret it."

He marched up to her and held her arms above her head with one hand and took hold of her chin with the other. Neither hold was gentle. Neither upset her, more the opposite. Shane squirmed on the bed and clenched her thighs to try to ease the aches in her clit and pussy.

"Stop it. You will *not* come unless I say so, and the way you're behaving at the moment, there's fat chance of me letting you. The spanking I'd give you for that, plus your cussing, wouldn't be for pleasure, I assure you. However, to go back to your question. Normal? Define normal."

As usual, he made a valid point. What was normal? "Happy, then? No monster in the closet or... Oh, help me here please, Sir. It matters."

"As far as I know, kitten, Jess is happy."

Shane let out a sigh. "I guess as a Dom you'd see the signs if she wasn't."

"I guess I would, and David certainly would."

Shane nodded and yawned. The events of the day, to say nothing of the previous week or so's happenings were catching up with her. "Sorry," she apologized. "It's not the company or the surroundings that's making me yawn. It's been a hectic few weeks."

"Come on." He dragged her onto her feet. "I'll show you where you're sleeping. We can talk tomorrow. Jess won't get back 'til mid-morning at the earliest."

"Yeah, sorry." With another yawn—and one last look around the dungeon—Shane let Ross lead her out of the room and back to his flat. Her self-imposed fast was sure looking like it would break soon. It couldn't happen quickly enough. She was ravenous, and not for food.

* * * *

"Do you want anything to eat?" Ross steered Shane back into the kitchen. "One sec." He disappeared and returned with her robe. "You're so tired, you're shivering." He helped her into the warm dressing gown and tied it around her waist. "I'll rephrase that. Sit down and let me get you some soup." He pressed down on her shoulders until she folded into a chair. "Two minutes."

It was less than that when Ross plonked a bowl of steaming, fragrant soup in front of her and added a thick chunk of what looked like homemade bread. "Eat," he said. "The soup I made, the bread is Kath's. Since she had her babies, she's going through an earth mother phase. There's no guarantee if it's as light as a feather or as heavy as a brick. It all depends on how many distractions there were when she made it."

Shane held a bit to her nose and salivated. It smelled amazing, warm, yeasty and mouth-watering. She bit into the doughy center and sighed. "Oh, no distractions. Or whatever they were, tell her to have them again. This is amazing." She spooned some soup into her mouth. "And so is this. Are you a chef in vanilla-land?"

Ross blushed and Shane stared at him. "You are?"

He shook his head. "Not now. I was for a while, before I got fed up working evenings instead of playing. Now I sell insurance." His eyes twinkled, daring her to disagree.

"You do not." She ate some more bread and soup. The cold, hungry, shivery feeling had disappeared. She still had a shivery feeling, but this one was warm, welcome and tingling in all the right places.

"True, I don't. I'm an investment analyst."

"Blimey, not much different then. Do you enjoy it?"

"Yup, and it fits around my lifestyle rather than my lifestyle fitting around it. I have an office a few miles from here, and I can also work from home." He opened the shutter, just enough for them both to see the depth of snow on the window ledge. "Six inches and no stopping. Just as well I can work here."

Shane put her spoon down and used the last piece of bread to mop the bowl. "That was beautiful, thank you. Er, now I think I'll go to bed."

"Let your food digest first." Ross picked her up as if she was a featherweight, and carried her into the lounge. He sat down on the settee and settled her on his lap. "There now. Let's snuggle for a while." His hand was warm as he stroked her cheek and hair. Shane gave in to her desires and burrowed close to him. He represented safety, calm and comfort. She craved all of them.

* * * *

"Shane."

Someone was shaking her as the room spun and dark spots danced in front of her eyes. She tried to bat his hands away. They were hard and menacing, and shook her back and forth to an unheard rhythm. Whoever it was caught her hands easily, and held them fast. She struggled, but it was futile. For all the good she did, she might just as well have been a fly in a spider's web. Although she might have guile — sometimes — she didn't possess brute strength. Whoever he was, he had both.

He loomed over her, but his face was in darkness. All she could see was a glitter. His eyes? Why was the rest of him hiding from her? Who? Shane struggled and kicked out only to be stopped by what seemed like iron bands over her legs. She opened her mouth to scream and found it shut fast by another mouth firm against her lips.

That wasn't right. No way could she let him — let the faceless one — win. Monsters had to be slain, it said so in all the books. Monsters needed cutting down. Where was Jack the giant slayer when she wanted him? Or even her master.

No, no, not him, not Master. Master was a monster, no more monsters. Not now, not ever. Sir… Yes, Sir…

Shane renewed her struggles, gasping and sobbing at the same time. Her breath was erratic and her mouth hollow with a nasty metallic taste in it. Why her? Why now? Hadn't she suffered enough? Why was she held captive, and no one came to her rescue? Where was Sir? Not the Master… He wasn't right, but Sir? Surely Sir would aid her?

The slap to her face made her gasp and turn her head into something hard and unyielding. She was suffocated, couldn't catch her breath, no one would hear her, she'd die tied up and alone.

Damn it. Nooo.

"I want my Sir. I want him. Ross, Sir, I need you."
Did he hear her? Why would he? This was her
nightmare, not his. "*Sir, tell him no, tell him...*"

"Kitten, wake up. You're dreaming." This slap was
enough to flip her head back. It jarred and her neck
rocked back and forward. "Shane, kitten, do as your
Sir says. Now."

The timbre of his voice penetrated into Shane's
consciousness and she moaned. The panicky breathing
slowed and she gulped back her sobs.

"That's it, kitten. You're here with your Sir. Ssh...
Open your eyes now. Look and see where you are."

"Don' wanna." What if he lied? What if it was all a
big ploy to catch her and show her how silly she was
to think it was all over? "Why?"

"Kitten. You'll make me cross if you don't obey me."
It was definitely Sir. "Look at me. Now."

Shane opened her eyes somewhat reluctantly and
realized she still stared at a T-shirted chest. From the
corner of one eye, she noticed her robe was off one
shoulder and the belt wrapped around one of her
wrists and across one of Ross' ankles. She had no idea
how that had happened. Very cautiously, Shane
moved her head to stare up at the concerned face of
Ross.

"Sir." She clutched a handful of T-shirt. "Oh, my
God, Sir." She burst into noisy, cathartic tears. "Don't
let me go."

"No, kitten, I won't let you go," Ross said. "Cry it all
out." He slipped his hand under her bathrobe and
scribed soft, soothing circles.

How long they stayed like that, Shane had no idea.
Ross continued his soft stroking of her back and
nuzzled her hair as he murmured silly nothings to her

in a calm and steady voice. Eventually she shuddered, sniffed and hiccoughed.

"Better?" Ross handed her a fine lawn hankie. "Blow."

Shane gave a watery giggle. "On this? It looks expensive."

"It probably was, but, hey, it'll wash. My mum is a great one for every man carrying a proper handkerchief. I get three new ones every birthday and Christmas. I threatened to tie them together and use them for bondage."

Shane struggled to sit up, and stared at him. "You didn't?"

"Uh-huh." He kissed her forehead. "She said she'd wondered when I'd think of that. No flies on mum. She's a Domme and according to my subbie dad, a bloody good one. He calls her 'My Lady', and she calls him petal."

"Petal?" Shane vaguely remembered Ross' stevedore dad. A petal he wasn't—more like the whole flower, or even the bush.

Ross shrugged. "Works for them, kitten. How you feeling now? Ready for bed? I was going to turn on the electric blanket, but I was side tracked."

"By a shrieking, screaming, crazy subbie?"

"By wanting to care for my lovely, brave subbie who fought as if the hounds of Hell were snapping at her heels."

His words cosseted her and gave Shane the strength to know what to do next. She slid off his lap, very slowly slipped the robe off her body and pushed it away. Then she knelt at his feet, put her head into his lap, kissed his groin gently and forced herself not to jump when his cock twitched under her touch.

"Sir?" Shane lifted her head to look at him. His dark eyes shone in the lamp light and his expression was full of something she daren't hope was care rather than compassion.

"Kitten?"

"Sir, I'm scared to sleep alone. What if the nightmares come back?" She didn't think it lightly. She hadn't had one for years, and knowing Ross was close too and ready to look after her made it almost a certainty her sleep would be nightmare free. However, she might need all the ammunition she had, so she'd use it.

"Ah, kitten, if I sleep with you, sleep won't be the only thing we do."

Shane bowed her head. "I'm sort of counting on that, Sir. Ross, please be a Dom for me. My Dom."

Chapter Nine

Now what the hell does she mean by that? Ross mulled over Shane's words. "In my bed?" he prodded. "As my sub?"

She gulped. "If that's what you want, Sir."

He could see the inner battle she was having with herself reflected in her expression. "We won't just have sex. You know that, kitten. There will be more than sex involved."

"I know, Sir. I accept that, and I'll be happy to do whatever my Sir wants."

"Upsadaisy then." Ross waited until Shane scrambled to her feet. "Last door on the left. Bathroom inside. Fresh toothbrush in the cabinet. I'll give you five minutes and expect to see you naked on the bed on your back, legs apart and your arms holding the headboard. I seem to remember I owe you some cuss word spanks."

She paled then grinned. "Yes, Sir, I remember."

It took a lot of determination not to say what the hell and follow her straight away. Ross counted off the minutes before he switched off the lights in the kitchen and lounge and made his way to the master bathroom. There he showered and cleaned his teeth, before slipping on a clean pair of leather trousers and a tight black waistcoat. He might as well set the scene. After making sure he had enough condoms in his pocket, Ross walked toward his bedroom. The door was half open and through the gap he could see Shane in the position he'd requested. It emphasized her beautiful breasts and made her nipples stand up. Her pussy, sadly still covered in hair, was a mound that called to his primal, dominant self, and the trickle of her juice that slicked her legs a turn on he couldn't—and wouldn't—ignore. Once he knew she'd seen his attire and by her erratic breath, accepted it was arousing her, Ross stripped with more haste than finesse and stood at the bottom of the bed.

"Like I said, kitten, we won't just have sex tonight if I stay here."

"No, Sir, I understand."

"Good." He pinched each nipple in turn, hard enough to make her gasp and writhe at the sting of pain he knew he'd inflicted.

"No, kitten. I know this for a fact and you'll find out very soon—not sex, and not subbing. We're going to make love."

It was worth all the pain of his excruciating arousal and his rock hard shaft to see the surprised, disappointed then joyous expression on her face.

There was no need for any more words on the subject. Ross lifted her legs to rest on his shoulders, bent his head and put his mouth to her pussy lips. She was so very wet, her taste gushed into his mouth as soon as he touched her. He swallowed the sweet feminine offering, nibbled around her clit and pulled the hard little nub into his mouth. Shane arched up off the bed and he pressed his hand on her tummy. No words were needed, and she flattened herself to the mattress once more with no more than a slight gasp and moan. He lifted his head long enough to praise her, "Good, kitten," before he renewed his assault, not only with his mouth on her clit, but also his fingers on her nipples. Her head thrashed from side to side, and her breath puffed out in tiny shallow pants.

"No coming...not before I say so." They might not be scening, but that he could abide by.

"Noo, ah, shit, yes, okay, one more spank, ten more, hell, twenty, but, Sir, please, it's been so long. Ahh, ahh..."

The keening sound Shane made shook him to the core. It might seem a contradiction in terms, but although Ross was a sadist, he wasn't cruel.

"One second, kitten, let me come inside you and feel you climax all around my cock." He moved to one side, donned a condom faster than he'd known it was possible and moved back between her legs. Her pussy and thighs were wet, and he knew her channel would be even more so. With no subtlety whatsoever, Ross pulled Shane down the bed until her butt was only just supported, lifted her legs onto his shoulders once more and thrust hard and sure into her pussy.

Three thrusts and she screamed and began to shake. Ross held her down firmly and continued to push. Her pussy was tight, her muscles clamped around him like a velvet vice, and his cock throbbed with his need to come. A film covered his eyes, making it hard to see clearly, his body stiffened, then red hot heat washed over his skin and into his very core as his climax hit him fast and furious, and he fell over the edge with a shout of completion.

Ross' legs and arms were jelly, and he found it hard to get enough air into his lungs to even wheeze. Shit, he sounded like an old man in his death throes, not a younger one after the best climax he'd ever experienced. Maybe they were one and the same? He let his body slump for a moment, until the shaking in his arms warned him he was about to fall, face first, onto Shane. She lay on the bed, her legs still over his shoulders with her eyes closed.

"More," she slurred. "When I recover in twenty years' time, can we do it again?"

"Ten, twenty, hell, two hundred. Times and years and...and...need to move, ditch the condom." At least he hoped that was what he said. It could have been gibberish, for all he knew. His ears were ringing and the only other sound he could hear was the double beat of their hearts. So at least they weren't dead then.

"Ditches. We're not in a ditch. Oh, I'm babbling, like a brook, in a ditch," she sniggered. "Oh, help, tell me to shut up."

"Shut up, kitten," Ross said obligingly. "Stay where you are. I'll be back."

He spent the bare minimum of time in the bathroom. Just long enough to wash, relieve himself and clean his teeth, before he went back to Shane, carrying a damp flannel and a warm towel. Heated towel rails were a godsend.

The lights flickered as he reached the bed and Ross started. Where had he put the flash lamp and candles? It was almost a given they'd lose power on a night like this. Resolutely he ignored the way the light ebbed and flowed and instead applied the washcloth to Shane's pussy and legs. She wriggled. "I can do that."

"So can I, kitten. It's an honor. Hold still." He dried her carefully, covered her with the duvet then dropped the towel and flannel on the floor. "I'm off to get candles and torches. The power will almost certainly go as the wind gets up. I won't be long." The lights flickered again.

"Self-fulfilling prophecy," Shane said as she snuggled down under the duvet Ross tucked around her. "Can you bring some water and the biscuits, please, Sir? I promise not to put crumbs in the bed."

"I can do better than that, kitten, just you wait and see."

* * * *

Ross made a beeline to the cupboard where he hoped he'd find at least one flashlight. He found two, plus a bag of tea lights and the emergency box of matches he'd put with them. When you lived in the back of beyond, it made sense to be covered for power cuts in bad weather. As the castle was at the end of the line, they were often the first to suffer a blackout and the last to have power restored. Hence the oil-fired Aga and open fires were not just nice to use and great to look at, they were more than practical. Those plus a few basic camping stoves meant he could cope until the emergency generator kicked in. As the generator *was* for emergencies only, and used more in the club than the apartments, it might provide basic light but little else.

He whistled as he took a basket from the pantry and filled it with crackers, cheese, pâté and a flask of coffee, as well as the water. It had been a long while since he'd felt so comfortable, and he realized with a jolt, so positive about his future. Whatever it was that was the skeleton in Shane and Jess' cupboard, he and Shane would work it out.

Ross stood in front of the open fridge door and considered the contents, before he added a couple of satsumas and a handful of grapes to his midnight feast. That would do. He ignored the wine. It was late, they were tired and he'd need to be up early the following morning to make sure the drive was clear of snow so cars could get up and down it. More than ever now he wanted Jess to get back and Shane to be satisfied that she could lay her demons or whatever to rest.

He looked out of the window as he made his way back to the bedroom and shivered. It looked like a scene from some snow laden movie where the hero trudged for days to rescue the heroine from the dragon in the castle. Except, Ross thought, amused at his fanciful thoughts, he was no dragon, and he'd rescued his fair lady from *outside* the castle, not in.

"Sustenance for the body," he said as he toed the door open. "We've done the soul bit for a while." *Not too long though, I hope, until we do some more.*

The bed was empty, the duvet thrown back over the crumpled sheet. Shane had turned down the lights to their lowest and created shadows and shapes in the room, opened the shutters and was kneeling on the window seat, with her nose almost pressed to the glass. Her naked body shone in the mixture of lamp and moonlight, and called to him in the most primeval way possible – as his mate.

"It's just like I imagined Christmas should look over here. So pretty." She shuffled along the cushions to leave space for Ross. "Look, all sparkly like diamonds and crystals dancing on the trees." She pointed outside and snorted. "Oh what do I sound like?"

Ross put the basket on the floor next to the fire and added another log to the flames. The fireplace and the open fire was something he relished, both in this room, and he often thought somewhat ashamed, also in the bathroom. It might sound decadent, but on some days, it was needed. Otherwise his bits might freeze to the porcelain.

He grabbed a condom and some wet wipes from their home on the shelf just inside the bathroom and he made his way to her. Ross peered over her shoulder and nuzzled her cheek, as he followed her pointing finger. "That bush there, looks like a giant cock, and the one over in the other direction is a witch," Shane said.

"She's covered in white then," Ross pointed out. "Only got black feet." The base of the tree was sheltered from the snow and a root protruded darkly out of the sea of white.

"Well she's a white witch then, in wellies."

"Fair enough. And the dragon is in the shadows," Ross said as he trailed his fingers down her spine and teased the hollow at the base before he circled the entrance to her arse. "Lurking before he makes his move to ravish the fair lady of the castle. And, oh, guess what?"

Shane twisted her head to look at him. "What?"

He pressed one digit inside her hole just enough to tease her, not enough to hurt. No lube was a no-no. To his pleasure, Shane pressed back a little. "Nice, but ouch."

"The hero has just reached you to save you from any danger." He hoped, there was still the worry of the white van and its contents, but that was neither here or now.

"Ohh, he has? How?" She opened her eyes very wide and fluttered her eyelashes. "Ohh, kind Sir, rescue me from danger? Save me, lordy, save me. How will you help me?"

She'd affected a deep southern accent, and even with its Aussie undertones, Ross reckoned it wasn't half bad.

"Like this." He moved to stand behind her and wedge his legs between hers. As she was kneeling on the seat, his weight moved her forward and she grasped the window ledge, for support, he guessed. However it was perfect for what he had in mind. Food could wait another few minutes. He had something much more interesting in mind than pâté and crackers. "Hold on there, perfect. No, don't turn round, just lift up a bit." He patted her bum, and Shane rose up so she no longer sat on her haunches. "Like I said, perfect. Now lean forward. The hero should have his reward, don't you think?" Without moving the digit that teased her nether hole, Ross slipped his other hand between her legs and two fingers into her pussy. Immediately the muscles which surrounded them tightened, and her wetness coated them. His cock responded to the invitation with alacrity, and brushed across his hand, her arse and slowly stroked the inside of her thighs.

"R...Ross? Sir?" Shane sounded doubtful. Immediately Ross understood. When his cock brushed her arse, it had indicated things that Shane wasn't sure of.

"Have you ever had a cock in your arse, kitten?" Try as he might—and if he was honest, he wasn't trying very hard—he couldn't stop calling her kitten. "Felt that sweet sting as it fills you there, and made you fly?"

"Sort of... It hurt not in a good way. It's a red." But he discerned a hint of hesitation in her tone.

"Red or amber. Tell the truth now." *Damned if I don't wish I had lube and could show her, just a bit how beautiful it'll be.*

The silence seemed to go on forever. A log slipped in the grate and they both jumped. Ross let his fingers slide slowly out of her arse and her pussy.

"Kitten? I need an answer or I'll tan your sweet arse."

Chapter Ten

Shane wriggled her fingers over the smooth wood she gripped and tried to dispel the sweatiness of her palms. This was her chance to see whether she truly was ready to be a worthy sub to her Sir. She knew deep down, now, even if Jess was a blubbering mass of humanity, she, Shane, deserved a chance of happiness, and she also knew it could be with Ross.

Speak or stay silent. Go for the spanking or admit to an amber reaction? Or be clever and have both? Shut up and have it put up. If it hadn't been so important she would have giggled at that thought.

"Kitten?"

Make my mind up time. She looked over her shoulders to stare at Ross. His expression was unreadable, but his features were taut and strained and even in the dim light, he looked pale. Now she had to work out how to show she wanted everything, one step at a time, and add a little light relief to the atmosphere.

Shane firmed her lips and mimed the zip closing movement again. Then she winked, returned to looking out of the window and wriggled her arse in, she hoped, a suggestive manner. If he didn't get her hint, she'd be snookered. After all, wasn't she doing as he decreed?

It was just as well they were miles from anywhere in the middle of a snowstorm. Her reflection stared back at her, outlined in the glass as clearly as if it was a mirror. Ross was equally noticeable, as he stood and stared at her thoughtfully and took a step back.

Shit, have I blown it? She opened her mouth to speak just as he nodded.

"So be it, kitten. Don't move an inch." He shifted out of the reflections in the glass.

Shut my eyes or keep them open? Bow my head or keep staring out of the window. Mind you, he said don't move. Oh fuck it, Shane, stop second guessing and just enjoy, or whatever.

Her inner lecture over, Shane continued to look at the snowy scene, which appeared over the reflection of her boobs. A movement showed behind her, and Ross once more loomed over her.

"My hands are cold and your arse is soon going to be rosy and glowing, kitten. This time, I'm going to warm you up myself, no crops or paddles. Although"—he held a plastic kitchen spatula up so she'd see it—"if you're a good girl, I might give you a few swats with this, just to introduce you to each other. Ready?"

Shane gulped and didn't care that if he looked at her inner thighs, they would be oh so wet now. Sod it. She was more than ready, even if apprehension was uppermost in her mind. It had been so long and the last time not... *Stop it now.*

"Yes, Sir."

In the glass she watched him nod and move sideways on to her.

"You know you can safe word out at any time, kitten?"

She loved how he ensured she was happy at every stage of their journey together. Because that's what it was, a journey, with, she hoped, a happy ending.

"I do, Sir. I'm green. Scared but green. This is the first time since, well since…" Her voice trailed off. "But," she continued in a stronger tone, "this is with you, so I'm happy and sure you'll do everything for us both that's needed." If he thought her words strange, he didn't say so.

"Then embrace the sting, kitten—five on each side to start."

Five? That's ten smacks. I thought it'd be one or t…. She didn't finish her thought as Ross swung his arm and slapped her right butt cheek. Sting was a misnomer. Stings were sharp and soon over. This pain spread through her. Sharp, yes, but soon over? Not at all. The awareness of harsh prickles and deep thuddy darts of throbbing sensation went on and on. Every few spanks he stopped and he ran his cold hands over her heated arse and stroked her skin. The contrast was almost unbearable. Almost.

"Ah, kitten, color?"

It would have been oh so easy to say red, or amber, and to chicken out. For several seconds she hovered between the two.

Honesty, remember. Honesty.

"Green, Sir."

"Good girl. Ready for the next ten?"

Shane bit her lip to stop a sob slipping out. She could take it, see how it all went before she decided if it was over and done with never to be tried again, or not. "Yes, Sir."

"Then count."

His hand met her skin, harder, more definitely and with a bite she'd not felt before. It took every ounce of determination not to shout, swear and scream at him to stop. With a depth of stubborn determination she hadn't known she had, Shane spoke out clearly.

"One, Sir." Then a second later. "Two, Sir." By the time she got to ten, she didn't hear herself or flinch as she waited for the next connection of his hand. No two swats landed on exactly the same place and the stings radiated all over her arse and into her very core. She was beginning to float.

"Such a beautiful sight, my kitten with a red rosy arse. Can my kitten take two more? This time with my swatter?"

He held the spatula in front of her face and stroked her cheek with it. It tickled, but Shane was under no illusion that it wouldn't feel like that if he swatted her arse with it.

"Are you ready to learn to embrace that as well?"

Why not?

"Yes, Sir." She was beginning to sound like a recording on repeat.

Ross didn't give her a chance to change her mind. Out of the corner of her eye she saw his hand fall downwards and the spatula disappear. She breathed out as slowly and evenly as she could as he placed the business end of the implement on her arse and held her steady so she didn't fall over with the force of his stroke.

It was oh so different. More thuddy, more definite and much more of an impact on her body *and* mind.

"Two more, kitten, yes?"

He could have said ten or one hundred and she would have given the same answer. The floaty feeling was divine. All for her, a sense of well-being and completion, nothing like the pain and horror she'd associated with it at one time.

"Yes, oh, yes."

He chuckled. "I think my kitten has discovered something about herself."

She nodded, too involved in her floaty happy sensations to do more. The last two swats were hard, but the pain *was* pleasure. He was correct.

The loss of contact as he stood back hit her hard. She moaned.

"Shhh, kitten, let me cuddle you now."

"Fuck me."

"Pardon? Do you know what you're saying?" Ross lifted her off the seat and swung her around to sit on it and face him. She winced at the pressure on her throbbing arse.

"Of course," Shane said, stung he'd think otherwise. "I want us to make love. Screw, have it off…" She yawned, giggled and covered her mouth. "I feel drunk."

"Subspace, kitten. So a drink and a cuddle first."

"'Kay. 'S'long as we do."

Bless her, she's out of it. Ross looked down at Shane as she gave him a slow smile and closed her eyes.

"You're mine, Sir Ross, all mine." She turned her head into his shoulder and exhaled deeply.

At least he thought she'd said mine. The words interspersed with yawns and sighs could have easily been something different. Fine? Dine? Wine? It had to, just *had* to be, 'mine'.

"That I am, kitten." Ross put Shane down on the bed as if she might break. She needed the sleep, and he knew enough about her to accept she'd bounce up and well…insist he kept his word?

God I hope so. Carefully, he pulled the duvet over her, and grinned as she rolled into the middle of the bed and hugged his pillow to her. As soon as he'd banked the fire, checked anything he might need to pleasure her if the opportunity arose and turned off the lights. Ross slid under the cover next to her. He pried her fingers open and began to drag the pillow away from her.

"No, he's mine." Her voice was determined and she tugged the pillow back toward her chest.

Ross gave up and used his arm instead.

Sometime during the night, he woke up to find himself with a dead arm and a furnace on top of him. A squidgy furnace that blew tiny puffs of hot air over his chest. He opened one eye and in the moonlight that streamed through the window saw Shane sprawled all over him and his pillow on top of her. No wonder he was sweating. He heaved the pillow off. Shane muttered something unintelligible and shifted on his chest. The next moment, she nuzzled his nipple and began to nip and tease the hard nub.

Ross held his breath and bit back a groan. Even if she was still asleep, it was such an erotic gesture, his cock was hard and pre-cum slid over it. The soft hand that cupped his balls took his breath away, and as Shane trailed her fingers up his cock to the bulbous head and began to stroke his pre-cum all over it, Ross began to recite the alphabet backwards in an effort not to come there and then.

"Kitten," he said in a strangled voice. It sounded so unlike him, even his mother wouldn't recognize it. Not that his mum would want to under these circumstances. She might be liberal and open-minded but there was such a thing as too much information and right there and then fitted that scenario perfectly.

Shane tightened her grip, and bent until her hair brushed his groin.

Ross groaned. "Shane... Wake up, kitten."

Boy, he thought he was the sadist, not the masochist. Her lips fastened on his dick and Ross decided he didn't give a flying fuck what he was. He was going to lie back and think of Australia, England, his cock in her arse, her tied and flying and all things in between.

Shane circled the head of his cock with her tongue, sucked hard and thrust the tip into the slit.

He stopped thinking altogether and let his inner senses take over. Every hair on his body stood on end, stung and tingled as he shook and trembled.

Shane gave a sultry laugh that curled around his heart and made it beat faster.

"Oh my, Sir likes this, doesn't he?"

The mattress dipped as she moved, and took him farther into her mouth. She tightened her lips then grazed her teeth along his length as she slowly released him.

Each time she repeated the action, more of his dick slid into her mouth and down her throat. Hazily, Ross decided he'd be tickling her tonsils before long, and hoped to hell she didn't gag. The familiar sensations of his balls tightening and the hard throbbing in his pulse points that spun through him as he was about to come began to hit him hard.

"Kitten, I'm so close to coming you need to decide to swallow or spit, and fast." He hoped to hell she understood the tortured words that his seemingly cotton-wool-filled mouth tried to utter. "Sweet sh... Now. Tell me now."

Her answer was to suck and tug ever faster.

Ross gave in and let his cum fill her mouth.

Shane sucked eagerly, milking every last drop as Ross shuddered and panted, before he finally quietened. Even then she continued to lick his cock, until Ross tugged her hair. Those gentle touches had gone from pleasure, to the pain only associated with being totally sated with no chance of anything else.

"Enough, kitten. Who's the sadist here?" He pulled hard on her handful of tresses he held until she gasped.

"You it seems, Sir. That is almost red."

"Rubbish." Ross didn't loosen his grip. "If this is nearly red, tell me how you coped earlier. Clothes pegs, for instance?"

"I was aroused," Shane said with dignity.

"And you're not now? Ohh such a pity, I'll put the bullet away then, shall I?"

"Eh?" She lifted her head, unheeding of any extra pain it must have caused, and stared at him. "Do not.... Er, please don't, Sir. I'll be a good little kitten and purr for you however you want." Shane crossed her eyes, screwed up her nose and mouth and gave a very creditable purr.

Ross laughed.

"Oh you'll purr for me all right. On to your back, now." The speed with which she obeyed almost made him laugh again, but he kept his face straight. Sassy subbie was an understatement. His kitten with claws was more fitting. "Now, little kitten, let's see how well you can purr, eh?"

He didn't wait for an answer before he leaned over and picked up the golden bullet vibrator he'd collected earlier. When he held it up for her to see, Shane wriggled dramatically and covered her eyes with one arm.

"Oh…my…Sir, I ahm at your merceee." She peered at him from under her elbow and winked.

"Minx. You so are, so you'd better remember that." He switched it on and stroked it across her clit, at the same time as he slowly teased her pussy with one long finger.

Shane lived up to his pet name for her and purred.

"Shoot, I like your mercy." She moved her hips in time to his slow thrusts in her channel, as she raised her butt to encourage him to stroke faster.

Ross lifted the bullet and she moaned her disappointment. "I need…"

"*No,* I need. I need you to listen and you to obey me. Don't come, kitten."

She mewled. "What?"

"You heard." He slapped her pussy mound, just hard enough to sting. "You come when I say, not before. And if I choose to leave you dangling all day, almost there but not quite, then that's what you'll do." He gave her three more stinging taps. Her skin suffused with a rosy glow and her eyes clouded, in the nicest way. With desire. Ross was experienced enough to know the signs. She was more than ready to come, her body would be so sensitive a feather over her clit would push her over the edge. "Do you understand, kitten?"

He waited for what seemed much longer than the few seconds it actually was, until she bit back a sob.

"Yes, dammit, yes, Sir."

Not quite right, but it would do.

"Then come, kitten." He put the bullet back onto her clit, and she screamed. Then shattered and fell apart in his arms.

Chapter Eleven

There was a very persistent fly buzzing in her ear. Shane muttered under her breath, and tried to sit up. The duvet or something had caught her and tangled her so she was stuck. After some effort she managed to jerk one arm up out of the covers and swatted her hand in the direction of that irritating noise a couple of times.

"Ooft." The buzzing stopped and restarted again, softer and more irregular than before.

Ooft? Flies don't ooft. Flies buzz and...oops. She opened one eye and twisted her head. Ross was snoring gently next to her, his head a few inches away on the pillow, his arm around her waist, and one leg thrust between hers. No wonder she thought she was stuck. His hard body almost covered hers, making even the slightest movement difficult.

She spent a few moments just looking at him, and letting the delicious memories of the previous day and night sink in. She really had played and made love to her childhood fantasy. Only now he wasn't a fantasy. He was the real thing. He looked so peaceful, but still so much a man in charge that her heart skipped a beat. If she hadn't discovered the urgent need to go to the loo, she could have stayed where she was, just looking at him.

Well no, not quite true, she admitted to herself. She'd be hard pressed not to twist the whorls of hair sprinkled across his chest around her fingers, and follow the arrow of them that lead ever downwards. And then… Shane groaned. It was no use creating hot and arousing scenarios in her head. She had to go to the loo. Very carefully she lifted Ross' arm off her middle and put in on the mattress.

He moaned and muttered something she couldn't hear and replaced it, via her breasts. Shane considered her situation. No, she couldn't wait for long. She took a deep breath, lifted his arm, edged carefully to one side so his leg no longer held her fast and rolled off the bed and onto the floor. The rug she landed on slid over the polished floorboards and her elbow met the edge of the bedside table with a clunk. She winced as pain—nasty pain—shot up her arm. "Ouch, shit and bugger, that hurts." She rolled onto all fours knelt up and rubbed the abused elbow.

"Shane?" Ross peered down at her. "As much as I love you on your hands and knees or kneeling at my feet, I can't see you there properly. Did we agree on that early morning protocol?" His voice was sleep filled and innocent, the glint in his eyes was not.

"Ha, ha, not." Shane scrambled to her feet and resolutely ignored the way he looked at her. As if he were the cat, and she a particularly tasty mouse.

"Out of interest, what are you doing down there?" Ross asked. "Come back to bed, we'll sort out what to do, when, later."

"I need." She waved toward the bathroom door, and he grinned.

"Then don't let me stop you." He swung his legs over the side of the bed. "I'll use the bathroom across the hall and meet you back here." He swatted her bum, and she growled.

"Oy."

Ross' laughter followed her as she walked as dignified as you could when you were buck naked and knew you had a drop dead gorgeous man watching your every move. She couldn't resist waggling her fingers over her head as she reached the en suite, even if she wasn't sure he was still watching.

The wolf whistle confirmed he was.

Shane grinned to herself and spent a penny, as her gran used to say, had the quickest shower ever and cleaned her teeth. By the time she went back into the bedroom, the fire was once more blazing brightly in the grate. She glanced toward the windows. The shutters and curtains were open on a scene from a Christmas card—the sort she'd drooled over as a kid, all sparkly diamonds and icy candles on the trees. It was hard not to clap her hands or high five the view.

Ross was propped up against the pillows, the duvet across his waist and a mug of something steaming in his hands. "Coffee. Yours is on the table. Come back to bed and snuggle."

"Thanks. Er, what time is it?" Shane had no idea where she'd put her watch. She clambered back into bed and picked up her coffee, to sip gratefully.

"Sex o'clock." Ross took her mug from her unresisting grasp and set it down next to his. "And we mustn't be late."

He rose over her almost before she had a chance to register how wet she was. His condom covered cock probed her pussy entrance, and Shane lifted her legs to rest her ankles on his shoulder. She loved the idea that he'd been primed and ready for her, and planned his strategy in advance.

"Ohhh, I have a visitor." She tried for a femme-fatale eyelash flutter and he winked.

"A very eager one, are you ready for him?"

"Oh yes." Her juices ran slowly over her thighs and gently down her legs.

"Oh my, you are, aren't you? Just as well really, he's more than eager." Ross pushed into her in one swift and sure movement, and immediately began a steady thrust and retreat. Shane matched his pace and he laughed softly and rested on one hand to use the other one to pinch each nipple in turn.

He wasn't gentle and Shane didn't want him to be. She reveled in the sting that ran through her from breasts to her clit and back again.

"Play with your nipples, kitten. Hiss and purr for me, show me how you like to tease yourself."

Ross moved his hand and pinched her clit, hard enough for her to hiss as he'd asked.

"Touch your nipples, kitten. I won't ask twice again." He withdrew almost to the head of his cock and waited for her to comply.

Shane wondered if it was worth defying him, just to see what would happen, but one look at his tight features decided that this wasn't the time to turn bratty. She took hold of her nipples between her thumb and forefinger and nipped each one hard. If anyone had told her she'd willingly inflict pain on herself, she would have poo poo-ed them and said they were crackers. But she did it gladly, her touch harder than anything Ross, or indeed Pete, had given her. The ends of her digits were white with the pressure she exerted. Of course Ross noticed.

"Sweet, kitten, you like that pain, don't you? Fly for me now." He pinched her clit so hard she arched up into him, and his cock filled her completely.

Shane screamed as spots flashed in front of her eyes and her every inch of her body flooded with pain, heat and the sense of Ross. Even through the condom he wore, she knew the second he came.

He shuddered and hissed between his teeth with a sharp indrawn breath. "Yes, yes, my kitten, oh yessss."

Then he slumped onto her, panting. His sweat slicked skin rubbed against her own, and her nerve ends stung. Every touch was like a hammer hitting those nerve ends, so much so even her teeth hurt. But she had no intention of asking him to move. The pressure was proof he was as affected by her as she was by him. It was indeed a sweet pain.

It could have been minutes or hours before he groaned, gasped and looked up at her.

"Hell, kitten, why didn't you tell me to move? I'm squashing you." He levered himself onto his hands and knees and withdrew from her with a gentle plop. Then he blinked.

"Fucking hell. Shit and buggery. Oh sorry, kitten, but we have a problem."

She knew already. Sticky semen coated her pussy lips.

Ross held the offending—and split—condom between his thumb and forefinger. "Bollocks."

"Well I guess they did have something to do with it." Shane couldn't summon up the energy to be angry or at that moment, even worried. "But, it's happened so now we wait, I guess."

"You sound awfully quiet for someone who might be up the duff," Ross said wryly. "How long until we know?"

"Ah, now there's the rub." Shane wondered why she didn't feel more embarrassed talking about her time of the month. But then after they'd shared what they had, it was a nothing to talk about. Sadly not a nothing to worry about once she got her head around the enormity of it. "I am so irregular my gynae lady said I was a bit like that trick question, what's easier to predict, who wins the ashes or when I come on. We decided it was who wins the ashes by a mile, and neither of us follow international blokes cricket. So, it could be anytime in the next five weeks, or well…" Her voice trailed off. "I could not."

Ross was silent for a moment. "And you're okay with that? It's your body, kitten, and I'll abide by what you decide." He got off the bed and walked toward the bathroom. "I'll dispose of the culprit."

He disappeared and Shane stared after him, nibbled her lip and tutted under her breath. Not a tut-tut how dare you noise. More a hmm, and how do I answer that? As much as she liked the idea of little Rosses or Shanes running around, she didn't want that yet. Hell, they'd only spent a few hours together. It was much too soon to be thinking of children. She had to get her head around a potential Dom/sub relationship first. If things progressed, that would be one of her first decisions, she was sure. Okay, even though she knew that would be a yes, it would be hard enough to learn what they both needed without morning sickness, a growing belly and heartburn.

However on the other hand, she didn't believe in the day after pill. It wasn't for her. Even if they could have got hold of one. As far as she knew, there was no chemist nearer than the small town near her hotel, and there was no way she'd expect Ross to chance his luck on that road. So wait and see it would have to be.

"What time is it?" Ross reappeared carrying a damp flannel and a towel once more. "Open up."

Shane winked and opened her mouth.

"Don't tempt me, kitten. You need your mouth washed out for your language yesterday."

She shut her mouth hastily and opened her legs, strangely shy when Ross performed the oh-so-intimate act of cleaning her up.

"There you are. All clean and cozy." Ross lifted her up out of the bed and stood her on the rug. This time it didn't slip. Typical, it only played up for her. "Ten o'clock. Judging by the depth of the snow, I don't see David and Jess getting back before mid-afternoon, if then. So what say you—we—go and get breakfast, and then talk?"

If he was trying to put her at ease, he wasn't succeeding. "Nope. It's snow angel o'clock. If you can find me some old joggers and wellies, let's go and make snow angels and a snowman. Then we'll talk and have breakfast." *And hopefully he'll know what to say.*

"Should you?" Ross looked doubtful. "You know, just in case?"

"*Argh...*" Shane threw a pillow at him. "In case? What, that you get snow down your neck? Count on it if you go on like that. Shrivel your dick and need me to resuscitate it? Oh yes please, Sir, as long as you stop being a prick."

Had she gone too far? Tough. It had to be said. Ross narrowed his eyes and stared at her. Shane knew a moment of worry, and the pulse in her neck throbbed its rhythm in double time. Then he gave a very reluctant sounding laugh.

"I was a bit, wasn't I? Sorry, kitten, macho male moment. Bear with me. To my knowledge, I've never been a prospective father before."

"We don't know that you are now," Shane said tartly. "And if you are, it's not even peanut sized, so no need to get all gooey and daddified. I don't want a Daddy Dom. I want a Ross one." She stopped speaking and put her hand on her forehead. "Busted, but I've got to add, as long as you want me. But I need to know… Why did you decide not to play properly, Sir. I would have done it, you know. If you ask, I'm happy."

"I know and I thank you. But we've time enough. I'd rather go slowly and have you with me every step of the way. Red was never my favorite color."

Shane smiled. "Nor mine. So what now?"

* * * *

After a pleasant, cold and damp hour or so making a snowman, angels in the snow and bombarding each other in an impromptu snowball fight, Shane and Ross sat cuddled together on the settee in front of yet another roaring fire, sipping mugs of homemade soup as they listened to the crackle and hissing of the logs as they burned. The joint shower had of course ended in Ross taking Shane up against the wall, until she'd slumped in pleasure. A phone call from the absent Jess and David had confirmed the roads still weren't open and it wouldn't be until the next day at the earliest before they returned. As Shane had asked Ross not to mention her, he hadn't, but the enforced wait was dragging and it grated on Shane's 'let's get things sorted' mentality. But the expression put up or shut up, stopped her moaning her lot. At least she was with the man she wanted to be with. She looked up at him and grinned.

"One word from you — well, okay not quite, but you know what I mean — and I go to mush."

"Ha, some mush. You, my kitten, are the most ornery sub I've ever known and I love you for it. However, you've been so determined you need to see Jess first, I can contain myself for a few more days to let you do it. But then, watch out, I've a lot of Domming to catch up with." He ran his hand from her forehead to her chin, and down her neck. The feather-light touch was enough to make her pussy muscles tighten. Of course, Ross noticed and grinned.

"I so love how receptive you are to my touch, kitten. If your talk goes as you want it to, Shane, will you think about perhaps being properly mine? Partner and sub, and maybe one day soon take it all one step further. Oh, I know we've really only just met, but in another way, I think I've been waiting for you all my life. Ever since I saw a scrubby school girl with scraped knees peeking at us all, and following us whenever she could like a tiny kitten with claws. Why do you think I did so much skinny dipping?"

Shane giggled. "You were so worth peeking at. Why do you think I spent so much time falling off my surfboard? Every time you hauled me back on, I got tingles. Okay, I wasn't sure what they meant, but boy did I enjoy them. And once when I saw you jack yourself off, I thought… Well, if boys can, why can't girls? That was when I discovered how my clit worked. So I have to thank you for introducing me to self help. It's come in very…er, handy over the years."

Ross snorted. "Glad I was able to assist."

She took a deep breath.

"Sir, however my talk goes with Jess, I'm yours. I just need to know she's okay, and then I can let go of my past and move into my future with you."

Chapter Twelve

"Do you ever get that weird feeling that you're being dissected, discussed and hopefully not found wanting?" Ross asked the dark-haired man who stood next to him. "As in how Domly is your Dom, and how much brattiness can you get away with?" He nodded in the direction where two women sat together, glasses of wine in their hands and heads together, talking as fast as they could get the words out.

"As long as they're not comparing dick length or stamina, I guess we can cope," Ross said. "And if they're swapping stories of how many times they come in a night or hit subspace, let's hope to hell they're equal." Not that he and Shane had a lot of the subspace scenario for her to talk about.

Not yet.

"Yeah. And I'm a bit limited as to what I can demand at the moment." David sounded distracted. "Oh shit, forget I said that."

Ross nodded. "Said what? I didn't hear anything."

David punched his arm in a 'thank you' gesture.

"They're cooking something up between them."

Ross was sure about it. Every so often one of their subs glanced in the men's direction and giggled. Several times Jess circled her hands in the air, as if she was describing something important and Shane nodded. Then they high fived each other and emptied their glasses before refilling them again.

"Scarily, I agree." David tapped his fingers on the chair arm as he acknowledged the truth in Ross' statement. His eyes crinkled as he looked at Jess. "Subs united should be banned — or at least supervised." He laughed, and both women glanced toward their men, with similar expressions of brattiness and apprehension on their faces.

Ross winked and Shane's worried look disappeared. She had never admitted out loud just how often she'd woken in the night, sweating and thrashing around, with the duvet twisted around her body. Or how she held onto him as if he were her anchor. He'd never pushed her to. The hollow cheekbones and the sunken eyes she'd sported were an indication of how worried she was and Ross had helped in the only way he knew. To be there, push her as far as he could BDSM-wise without breaking his promise and keeping her days — and evenings — busy.

It had been a tense few days, as the snow didn't shift, and the farthest they managed out of the castle was to the woodshed. Ross admitted the return of David and Jess to the estate had been a relief — as had the news that this time they'd gotten away with a defective condom. Even though the way her body reacted made Shane cranky and out of sorts, he could cope with that. A massage and a climax worked wonders.

He'd pretended he hadn't heard her whispered 'one day', when she told him that news. Although they had both promised, 'no secrets', some things had to wait to be discussed.

"Oh, ho, here they come." David rolled his eyes as the women stood up and walked toward Ross and David. "At least they both look okay." He'd confided his worry to Ross that chatting with Shane might not be the best thing for Jess, who would have some interesting news for them once Jeff and Kath were back from their holiday with their babies. Ross took this to mean more babies on the way.

Ross smiled as Shane walked up to him and sat down on a cushion at his feet. It wasn't something he insisted on, but something she liked to do, and he wasn't going to stop her. Even in jeans and T-shirt, the position suited her. She dipped her head and his cock twitched. The look of submission made him wish he could pick her up and carry her off somewhere private to show her how he felt toward her.

Mine.

"All right, kitten?"

"Oh, yes, Sir. Oh, and, Sir, Jess is happy for me to explain everything to you."

To his left Jess sat on a low stool and put her head in David's lap. Another hint of their changed circumstance? Normally she would also be on a cushion whenever they were in the club.

The day before Shane and Jess had met and chatted and Shane had then asked for them all to be in the club whilst she explained things.

"It's sort of fitting, Sir, and I want to show you I'm okay. That I really meant it when I said Ross, will you be my Dom."

Ross couldn't deny her that. Truth be told there wasn't much he could deny her, though he kept that nugget to himself. Shane was already enough of a minx.

"Are you sure, pet?" David's voice was low and full of concern as he spoke to Jess. "You know…"

"Oh yes, Sir." In contrast, Jess' voice was clear and confident. "Let's bring it out into the open here and now. Because it's not just me that Poisonous Pete the Plonker affected. It was Shane and her family as well."

"Pete the…?" Ross looked from Jess then to Shane, who wrinkled her nose and raised her eyebrows.

"The Plonker," Shane repeated obligingly.

"I guess I do need filling in, as you so elegantly put it, kitten," Ross said. "Who on earth is Poisonous Pete the Plonker?"

"A wannabe Dom, who most certainly wasn't one, who pulled in and caught several wannabe subs, including yours truly," Shane said.

Ross picked up on one word that didn't fit properly into her sentence. "Was?"

"Was," Shane said firmly. "Sir, please don't interrupt."

He nodded and sat back in the chair as he played with Shane's hair. Her whole body relaxed as she leaned onto his legs once more.

"And this yours truly was caught as well," Jess added. "Gullible were us."

"He took great pleasure in blindfolding and tying his subs up and leaving them, making them think he'd cleared off, when in fact he was in the next room or even, I believe at times, in the same one, jerking off to their cries for help. Fucktard, and I *meant* to swear," Shane said fiercely. "I was lucky. I got away when he fell asleep, because his knots were crap, but my brothers rescued Jess when they went to sort him out on my behalf."

"By then, his knots weren't crap," Jess said with feeling. "I know 'cause I didn't half try to get out of them. But the boys loosened them and now I know they stuck around to make sure I got away. But talk about knights in shining armor—well, okay, bikers' leathers. They met up with me a few days later and told me they knew what had happened, that he'd done it before and wouldn't ever again. Like I said, talk about naïve and a first class idiot. And telling myself that he was a clever, manipulative shit doesn't help very much.

"I'll kill the bastard," Ross said and stood up to pace the room. "Where is the little worm?"

"You're too late, Sir. Someone beat you too it. No names, no pack drill. I'm not getting anyone in trouble for helping him to rid the world of himself."

"Then, well...let's just say, they were more than mere men the way spirited me out of there, and telling me it was over forever helped me to get on an even keel. Mind you," Jess lifted her head to grin at David, before she nuzzled his crotch unselfconsciously. "It took my Master to make me whole again."

The look that passed between them was so intimate, Ross felt an intruder. Beside him Shane stirred uneasily. He glanced down at her. "Kitten?" he asked softly.

"Sir, I want that."

He knew exactly what she meant, but he needed to spell it out and to hear her agreement. After what he'd heard, Ross was amazed Shane was even in the castle, let alone sitting as she was and talking about subbing for him. "All of it, kitten? Scening, playing, demonstrating in the club? Collar, marriage and all things attached?" *And children?*

She bit her lip, swallowed heavily, and the skin over her throat rippled. "All of it, Sir. I've been given the chance to change my life—to have what I unknowingly longed for all those years ago. And they do say you have to kiss some arseholes before you kiss your prince."

Epilogue

"Are you sure you want this, kitten?" Ross checked his scissors and knives were handy in case his quick release system failed, and stroked Shane's cheek. "You can cry red and no one will think any less of you."

Shane took a deep breath. She did want it — sort of. Or at least she wanted to try it. *To get the first time, I'm a virgin at this showing-myself-off-in-next-to-nothing-in-front-of-an-audience stuff over.* Letting Ross Shibari tie and rig her in private was one thing. That she'd come to love and hit subspace every time. However, to let him do it in front of an audience, notwithstanding one as small and intimate as his fellow Doms and their subs, even if they were all now friends, was something else entirely.

"I'm sure, Sir. Green, Sir." *But please let's get it over and done with before I throw up or something stupid.* It wasn't the play she was worried about. It was letting herself go in front of others. For so long she'd kept a strict hold on her emotions, that even to Ross it had been hard. But to people who were in the lifestyle, who lived it... Well, that wasn't as easy.

Ross took her chin in his hand. "You better mean it, kitten, or once we're out of here I'll spank you so hard you'll not be even able to sit on a cushion in comfort."

Shane giggled nervously. "Then if I have to lie on my tummy, it'll make it easier for you to get to my arse then, Sir."

"Brat." He smacked the offending arse, which was covered only in Ross' favorite scarlet thong. "Okay, I trust you, kitten."

"And I trust you, Sir."

"Then let's make you fly."

Their audience sat outside the circle of light that enclosed them. As Ross worked, tying his ropes around her, talking to her softly and giving her all the encouragement she wanted, Shane forgot the watchers. All that existed was Ross, and how he affected her.

With each turn of the rope she sank further into their own world. The only sounds she heard was Ross' voice, the rustle of rope on rope and their breathing.

"I'm lifting you now, kitten. Color?"

"Green, Sir." Her world tilted as Ross hauled her upwards and gently set her spinning. Shane let her mind float and her senses take over. This was her world and she loved it, and the man who held her future in his hands — or ropes.

Shane Donoghue was where she wanted to be at last. Now she had to make sure Ross understood she was one hundred percent honestly happy and ready to do more. The swing — rig — she wasn't sure what to call it, and in her endorphin-induced state she wasn't inclined to try and fathom it out, moved gently under her weight.

"Green," she said again and grinned as Ross narrowed his eyes then nodded.

"Can you fly for me, kitten? Literally and mentally. Purr and show everyone how good this is." He leaned forward and held the ropes steady whilst he pressed several nipping kisses along her neck. "Shall I give you a helping tap, I wonder?"

Shane held her breath. It wasn't a question. Ross tugged her hair so she looked him in the eyes. At that moment he was all out a Dom. A man in control of himself and her, and he wore his authority easily.

"Shall I offer the opportunity to another Dom?"

In her state of heightened awareness, Shane couldn't identify the emotion that flooded her. It wasn't fear, but neither was it pleasure. She'd never wanted to be shared and hadn't thought Ross wanted it either, but he'd have a reason for what he said, surely?

"Answer me, kitten."

Her stomach was full of butterflies as he set her in gentle motion again and she swallowed and cleared her throat before she could answer. "It's up to you, Sir."

"It is, isn't it."

The pat on her bum as he spun her in a lazy circle did no more than sting a little, but it concentrated her mind on him, instead of her reaction to his words.

"So." Ross spoke slowly. "Then I don't share. Never. You're all mine."

"Yes, Sir." The relief was disproportionate to what he'd allegedly considered. A few swats to her arse wasn't really sharing, but she was glad the idea was a no starter, anyway.

The next pat as she swung past Ross was harder and the next, harder still. Shane moaned in pleasure as the stings flowed through her body. Tied and swinging around her Sir as he concentrated only on her, she began to ignore everything except how he made her feel.

"Shane, I need you. I need more." He stopped the rig spinning and held her in one place with his hands clamped firmly on her arse and her clit at the height of his mouth. Now she understood the way his Shibari creation circled her breasts and separated her legs.

Somehow she knew what he meant by more. She ached to experience his touch everywhere. His lips on her clit were a welcome balm to her heightened state of arousal. When his tongue probed her channel she moaned and when he suckled on her clit, she sighed in ecstasy. Did he know what he did to her?

Stupid question, of course he did.

The first tiny nip was enough to send every sense on high alert. The harder bite made her tense her muscles and the subsequent laving of her mound and perineum, sent goosebumps dancing over her skin.

Shane's senses were spinning just like the rigging, as Ross continued his ministrations. Her body was on fire, and her climax so close she began to shake. He lifted his head and blew on her clit.

"You're not going to come, kitten. Not yet. You see, I'm going to lower you, and then I'm going to fuck you senseless. I need to feel your warm cunt around me, to listen to your little mewls and purrs as you hold me inside you. And you'll come for me again and again and again when I say so and not before. Am I right?"

"Y...yes, Sir." Even though a few moments earlier she had considered herself totally sated, now, merely listening to his voice made her wetter and aching for him.

As he lowered her, Ross never took his eyes off her. Ripples of excitement danced over her skin as she realized he wasn't going to untie her. She might not be able to move, but every part of her was still easily available to his touch.

He stripped and stood looking down at her with eyes that were cloudy with desire.

Shane's mouth went dry and she swallowed several times. "You are magnificent, Sir." To her amusement, Ross skin suffused with color.

"Hell, kitten, I could come by just looking at you, and you say something like that. I feel humbled."

"I'd rather you felt me, Sir."

Ross laughed. "Oh, my pleasure." He slid over her and into her in one long smooth movement and she moaned.

"More."

He smiled and began to move. With each stroke he withdrew his cock to the tip, and then thrust deep inside her. Shane loved the sensations of being stretched—of her Master over her, inside her, and taking her deeper into ecstasy. Her pussy was soaked, her legs damp and she floated in that special space where he sent her.

"Let go."

She did and forgot everything and everyone, except his voice and her release.

How long she hovered in subspace she didn't know, but gradually Shane became aware of the fact she was no longer tied or in the air, but sitting on his knees with his arms around her, her head on his naked chest, and snuggled in a warm fuzzy blanket. His chest hair ticked her cheek and his even breath stirred her hair. Somehow she knew the room was empty, apart from themselves. What they had just experienced was much too personal and precious to share.

Ross' voice surrounded her, as he told her just what his feelings were.

"I love you. You know that, don't you kitten? You're all I'll ever want. You are mine. My partner, my kitten, and soon I hope, my wife."

"Oh…yes…" Somehow she managed to formulate and speak the words.

"Then, my kitten." Ross held her chin in one hand. "Please look at me."

Shane opened her eyes and gazed into his. The knowledge that the love that shone out of them was all for her was very special.

"Yes, Sir."

"So, may I collar you?"

Ross held out a fine silver chain with a heart-shaped lock. Shane nodded, and he frowned. His command to her all that time ago filled her.

Vocalize.

"Yes. Oh yes, Sir."

Very carefully he fastened the collar around her neck and kissed her.

Shane sighed with happiness. She was cherished, in a bubble, cocooned by his love and tenderness.

His.

About the Author

A multi-published author of erotic romance, Raven lives in Scotland, along with her husband and their two cats—their children having flown the nest—surrounded by beautiful scenery, which inspires a lot of the settings in her books.

She is used to sharing her life with the occasional deer, red squirrel, and lost tourist, to say nothing of the scourge of Scotland—the midge. As once she is writing she is oblivious to everything else, her lovely long-suffering husband is learning to love the dust bunnies, work the Aga, and be on stand-by with a glass of wine.

Raven McAllan loves to hear from readers. You can find her contact information, website details and author profile page at http://www.totallybound.com.

Totally Bound Publishing